Rachael's
Apocalypse Diary
Smiling Flu Book 2

Len M. Ruth

Ruthless Press

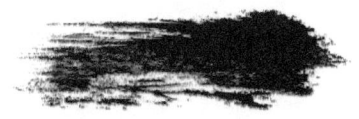

Editor's note:

This is a diary, obviously. In the process of getting it ready for publication, I had a lot of tough choices to make. On the one hand, I wanted it to be a smooth, polished experience for you, dear reader. On the other hand, I didn't want to erase Rachael's unique voice. Though she's a nuclear engineering student, she's also a young millennial writing in her diary. Taking that into account, I did my best to edit Rachael's diary with a light touch. I think the roughness of her prose conveys the danger surrounding her.

Further, she wasn't the kind of woman who marked off a calendar every day, and once her phone died, she had no way of knowing the date. Thus, I had to find a way of letting you know time had passed. How much time? We can only use the clues she left us.

I hope you enjoy reading Rachael's Apocalypse Diary as much as I did.
Len Ruth

Editor's note:

This is a diary, obviously. In the process of getting it ready for publication, I had a lot of tough choices to make. On the one hand, I wanted it to be a smooth, polished experience for you, dear reader. On the other hand, I didn't want to erase Rachael's unique voice. Though she's a nuclear engineering student, she's also a young millennial writing in her diary. Taking that into account, I did my best to edit Rachael's diary with a light touch. I think the roughness of her prose conveys the danger surrounding her.

Further, she wasn't the kind of woman who marked off a calendar every day, and once her phone died, she had no way of knowing the date. Thus, I had to find a way of letting you know time had passed. How much time? We can only use the clues she left us.

I hope you enjoy reading Rachael's Apocalypse Diary as much as I did.
Len Ruth

Entry 1

I hate diaries. But I feel compelled to document my struggle to survive. Jesus. That makes me sound like a pompous jackass. I have no idea what day it is, so I can't date my entries. I guess it's been about three weeks since the power went out. Thank God it isn't winter, or I'd be a popsicle and not writing this. I'll have to find some way to keep track of time in this little notebook, but that's for another time. Oh, yeah, my name is Rachael.

Before all this, I watched a lot of apocalypse and disaster movies, and not one of them showed the crawling carpet of wiggling brown insects I have here. Also, there's the smell. The movies might mention the smell, but then the characters go about their business as if they were in a pine-scented forest. Let me tell you, it's not like that. At the beginning of the outbreak, the government did a pretty good job of getting the sick to the hospitals and the dead to the morgues. Later on, though, not so much. I've got a third-floor apartment (well, it is... was my brother's) across from the hospital. We watched the National Guard put up giant tents in the parking lot after they towed all the cars away. I bet they could fit a hundred beds in each one. People lined up for blocks trying to get in, but within a day, no one else was. I guess the tents were already full.

My brother got sick a couple of days later. He made me put a gallon of water in the bedroom and told me not to come in. I knocked every couple of hours to check on him. On the second day, he stopped answering. I'm sorry, I just can't talk about what he looked like or how hard it was getting him out of the apartment. It's not that I'm sentimental about his body. It's just a meat vehicle for the soul. I miss him a lot. Anyway, I started all this to tell you about the roaches. They started showing up a few days after the smell got really strong. I try not to imagine the bodies in the other apartments, the food rotting in the fridges and sinks, hungry pets dying next to their owners. The roaches showed up around the sinks. Just a few at first. That pissed me off. I keep this place very clean, even now that the water is off. When the smell in the building started making me gag, they showed up in force. Hundreds, thousands, scurrying across every surface in the apartment, including me! You're probably wondering why I'm still here, right? There's still food, and some water, more than I can carry, more than I dare leave behind. I'll need it. Plus, I figure if I went walking down the street with a bag of food and water, a nineteen-year-old, alone, well, the best thing that could happen is they'd steal my food. I don't want to think about the rest. Better to sit tight 'til supplies run out, or who knows, maybe someone out there can still fix this mess.

Anyway, the roaches. They're so bad I actually punched holes in the ceiling and hung the bed from ropes so they couldn't crawl up the bed frame and crawl into my mouth while I'm sleeping. I am—I mean, I was a sophomore nuclear engineering student, so I'm pretty handy. Now, I look down in the morning, and for just a second, I think there's a brown carpet on the floor before I realize it's moving. Yesterday I taped a sheet to the ropes over the bed after they started dropping down on me through the holes in the ceiling. The smell is so bad I gag all the time now. The whole city stinks, but the building is worse, so instead of just opening the window to empty my crap bucket, I left it open all day. Mistake! I thought the roaches were bad. They're nothing compared to the flies.

Entry 2

I have no idea what's going on in the world. From the looks of it, nothing. There's no TV, or radio, or internet, or anything to tell me whether to stay put or get out. So, with food and water starting to run low, I got out. I left my brother's apartment in DC yesterday on foot. I've seen a few people. When I got up the bravery to yell to a guy on the other side of the street, I asked if it was over and if there was a cure. He just shook his head and kept going. He had a red bandana over his mouth like an old-time bandit in a cowboy movie, as if that was going to do anything. Not for the smell, and not for the virus, just a ridiculous placebo.

Once you get to the open places, the smell of death is almost tolerable. Anyway, I walked out of the city at night because I thought I'd be less of a target for someone wanting to steal my stuff. Maybe I was right, but there were so few candles burning in windows, so few signs anyone else was left alive, that I'm not sure it was worth it for how scared shitless I was. The city was totally quiet. No cars, machines, planes, people, air conditioners, nothing. What the city does have is the dead, and the things that eat them, and the things that eat those things. It was too dark without the streetlights and car headlights to make much out, but damn, did I hear stuff. I'm talking mostly about rats here. They don't tell you about the rats in apocalypse movies. Oh sure, they throw one in here and there for a nice jump scare, but they don't show the teeming mass of vermin like there was in DC (and I'm not talking about the politicians). Trash bags that piled up after the trucks stopped coming—were moving. Whole crinkling black mountains wiggled in the moonlight. You could hear them chirping, squealing, and probably fucking inside the trash. They ran up and down the steps of houses, in and out of car windows, and sometimes right across my feet. Millions of huge rats rule that city now.

I saw a couple of dogs too. They were scary at first, but I think they were scared of me too. One, a cute little white terrier, grabbed a rat and shook it side to side. The rat's head cracked on the sidewalk. Then the dog just ate it right there like it was nothing, totally normal, just a regular bowl of kibble.

I'm heading south, away from the city, on 95. I figure it'll be the easiest walking. And I'm going to have to get somewhere warm before winter. Somewhere I can get food and water. What I'm really hoping for is to find out this thing mostly happened around DC. Maybe I'll start seeing cars without corpses in them, you know, driving around. Then I'll hitch a lift into a town with food and electricity, get a job, and live happily ever after. It could happen, right? Today I'd just settle for a roll of toilet paper. See, I spent last night in the back of a truck full of potato chips. It was a blessing because I was pretty hungry. The less said about the way I felt this morning, the better. Anyway, I really need a roll of toilet paper. They don't tell you about that either.

Entry 3

Water is a big problem. I started searching cars along the highway for sealed bottles of water on the first day. I hit the jackpot too. I found almost a full case. That was what? Four days ago? Walking is thirsty work. I keep looking for a car with no bodies, keys in it, and a charged battery. Might as well be looking for a unicorn. I don't know how to hot wire a car, or drive one either for that matter. DC had great public transportation, and driving just didn't seem that important—then. But I mean, now that there are no other drivers, how hard can it be?

Anyway, water. It's been a dry summer here. I wish I had a map. That's another thing no one ever really thought about. I can't say for sure I've ever held a paper map, except the ones they give you at theme parks to find the rides. Like everyone else, I just used my phone. Dead battery. And even if I could charge it, I'm not sure that would matter. I bet a million dollars there's no service anywhere anymore. I just made myself laugh. A million dollars. It's all useless paper now. How 'bout I bet a gallon of clean water instead? At this point, that is worth a million dollars.

As I get further from metro DC, there are fewer cars. That means fewer chances to find supplies. I need to get off the highway and take the surface roads south. There's probably more water and food, and who knows, maybe even people. People who will talk to me, help me. There's probably more danger, too. Paranoid much? Every time I hear a car (yes, there are still some cars driving around), I hide. I'm afraid they'll shoot me, take my stuff, maybe even eat me. Well, maybe not that last thing. There's not many people left, so there's still plenty of stuff lying around. I'm getting pretty sick of potato chips, though. I crammed my bag full when I left the chip truck. Speaking of that, I did find some toilet paper in the trunk of a car, lots of it, and whiskey, and cigarettes. Who stuffs their trunk full of toilet paper, whiskey, and cigarettes? Makes no sense. Why would someone hoard all that and not food and water? There were no corpses in that car, but no keys either. I slept in the back seat last night. I figured there was probably no virus if there were no bodies. Not sure how long the virus lives on stuff, so as long as I'm not sneezing tomorrow, I'm good—maybe. Anyway, wish me luck on the water front (see what I did there?).

Entry 4

In the apocalypse movies, they don't really tell you about the silence. Okay, yeah, they kinda do, but not the deep unbroken silence that stretches out around you, squeezes in on you, and makes you feel more alone than you've ever felt in your life.

I left the highway two days ago and found this little house by a little lake. I've been spending my time boiling lake water on the little wood stove, then putting it in any container I can find, then drinking the rest. This wouldn't be a bad place to stay except for the silence. It's driving me crazy. At night, you can hear the house getting older, falling apart. Every little sound means that this is all that much closer to dust. It's just an occasional click of wood on wood in the walls. A little creak to make you wonder if something's there... or someone.

It's funny, I haven't heard any people. You'd think they'd flock to a place like this, plenty of water and shelter, not too far from the highway. There are cottages all around the lake, but no people. Are there so few of us left? I thought it would get better when I got away from the city. At least it smells a lot better. There's no sound of birds or frogs, just boiling water and creaking wood. I wish there was someone to talk to. I'm worried I'm starting to get a little nutty being alone so much. It's been too long since I had a conversation with another human being. I'd talk to myself, but the silence feels impenetrable, sinister. Maybe I've read too much Poe, Lovecraft, and Stephen King. I wish those guys could be here to see this. Boy, did they get it wrong. Anyway, there's not a ton of food here. Enough for a day of walking, or two days of resting. I think I'll be on my way tomorrow before the quiet drives me insane.

Entry 5

Holy shit, I'm sick. My stomach cramps are so bad I can't stand up. I don't know why. It started this morning after I ate some instant oatmeal from a packet I found. It might not be the oatmeal, though. Those don't really go bad. I've been checking the expiration dates on everything. I was going to leave this little house by the lake after I ate, but then the cramps started. Then the throwing up started, then diarrhea. I'm too weak to get to the lake and fill the bucket I use to make the toilet flush. The whole house stinks something awful.

I wish there was someone here to help me, or even just someone to talk to, someone to tell me it's going to be okay. It's terrifying. I managed to clean up most of the puke from the kitchen floor, but the cramps got so bad I had to stop. Now there are ants. It's so stupid, me worrying about ants in the kitchen of a house I was going to abandon anyway. In my old life, before all this, I was a neat freak. My brother used to say, "Old habits die hard." I guess that's true. I wish he was here. I miss him so much, and my mom, and well, people, I guess. It's funny, I never used to be much of a people person, but now every day, the loneliness gets worse.

My stomach hurts so bad. If it's not the food, maybe it's the water. Maybe there's something wrong with the water from the lake. I've been boiling it, but maybe not long enough? Or, shit, I didn't even think of this, but what if it's a chemical contaminant? As a nuclear engineering student, I should have thought of that. I was studying to make chemicals, compounds, and processes my bread and butter. Now, fuck, they might be *in* my bread and butter. Could be why it's so quiet—why there are no birds or frogs. If it is, then, depending on what the chemical is, I'm dead. I'm getting dehydrated from the throwing up and diarrhea, and I'm just not strong enough to go looking for clean water. Just now, outside, I think I heard a car. But, as sick as I am, it could be a hallucination. No, no, it *is* a car, and... two doors closing, trying to be quiet, but I can still hear them. The window is open. Whispering. Steps on the porch. I have to go. Pray for me.

Entry 6

I was so sick all I could do was crawl out of the kitchen to the bedroom doorway where I could see the front door. It opened slowly, quietly, and a man with a salt and pepper beard was standing there with a little girl, maybe four years old.

"Oh God," he said, covering his nose and mouth with his hand.

"That's yucky, Grampy," the little girl said.

The man put his hand on the doorknob to close it.

"Wait, please," I said.

"I thought you were dead. It smells like you are."

"I'm sick—"

He started to close the door again.

"Please, wait, it's not the flu. I think it's the water. Please, Mister..."

He closed the door.

"Grampy, why aren't we going to help that girl?" I heard the little girl say through the door.

"Because she might make us sick."

"But that's not right, Grampy. You always say that we should help people. It's the Christian thing to do. We're still Christians, right?"

"Shit. Nancy, we're Catholics, it's... we're... Sunday Catholics... ah hell." He opened the door.

I wanted to cry with relief, but I couldn't spare the water for tears.

"Can you walk?" he asked.

"I don't think so. I'm so thirsty."

"Ok, I'll get you some water. I'll leave it by the door. I'm not coming in there. Get to the door, and drink the water. Then we'll talk." He left the porch and took the little girl with him.

I did my best to crawl to the open door. As I dragged myself across the kitchen, I did my best to avoid the remains of my puke and the ants feasting on it. The outside air was fresh and good, and it made me feel a little better.

The man came back up to the porch with a sealed bottle of water. He twisted the cap and set it on the weathered boards in front of me.

I pulled myself up and rested my back against the doorframe as I drank. The wind made a shushing sound through the pines that surrounded the cabin.

"Easy now," he said as I chugged the water. "Breathe. Make sure you keep that down. It's too precious to waste."

I stopped drinking and took a few breaths. The water felt icy inside me.

"What's your name?"

"Rachael."

"I'm Jeremy, and this is Nancy," he indicated the little girl standing by a black SUV with a bunch of stuff strapped to the roof.

"Hi," I said, then took another drink of water.

"How long have you been here?"

"Just two days. Yesterday I got sick. I think it might be the water. I...after I got sick, I noticed that there were no birds, frogs, or anything like that. So I've been boiling the water, but now I'm thinking it might be some other contaminant." My voice was weak and pathetic. I didn't like the way I sounded.

"Where did you come from?"

"DC."

"That's where we were headed. I thought maybe the government would still be functioning there. Maybe there would be a Red Cross shelter or something."

"If there was anything like that, I didn't see it," I said. I was already feeling better with the water in me.

Jeremy was quiet for a while. He looked around and listened. "You were okay before you got here?"

"Yeah, I was fine."

"Did you touch anyone? Remove any bodies from the cabin? Anything like that?"

"No, I swear."

"Did you eat any food that came from here?"

"Just a packet of instant oatmeal. It wasn't expired." I finished the water he gave me.

After a long silence, Jeremy said, "It *is* strange that there aren't any birds. I don't know if that means there's something wrong with the lake or something else. I'm not going to stick around to find out. Still, you seem like a nice enough woman, and even if I could find it in myself to leave you like this, Nancy wouldn't let me. How are you feeling now?"

"Better," I said.

He looked at me, considering something, then he sighed. "How long has it been since you had something to drink before this?"

"Yesterday morning."

"I'll give you some soda. It'll get a little sugar in you, something for your body to go on. If you can keep that down for an hour, we'll talk about what's next."

"Okay, thanks, Jeremy." He brought a can of Coke up to the porch. I did my best not to chug it. It was so good. I kept it down. We talked a little about our situation. I told him about my brother and what happened in DC. He told me a little about his daughter and how he came to be driving around with his granddaughter, looking for supplies.

"How are you feeling now?" he asked.

"Much better," I said.

"Seems like we both need a plan going forward."

"Yeah, there's got to be people or help somewhere."

"I sure hope so. Why don't you get yourself cleaned up? I think that would make you feel even better. Does the water work in there?" he pointed into the house. "No, I've been bringing up buckets from the lake."

"Well, I think you could use a dip in the lake. Even if you can't drink it, it's probably safe to wash." Jeremy looked me up and down, but not in a creepy way. "Also, a change of clothes if you have it."

"Yeah, just one, though."

"Well, maybe rinse those in the lake, too, then. I'll give you a ride out of here if you're still not sick after all that."

"Thank you, Jeremy." I was so relieved I sucked in a sob. Hey, it's not that I'm a weepy woman, you know, the kind that turns on the waterworks over every little thing. It's just that I thought I was going to die in that shitty little cabin.I froze my tits off washing up in the lake, but I did feel better afterward. And after putting on some fresh clothes, I was a new woman. The cramps still dropped me to the ground a few times, but they were growing weaker.

Now I'm writing as we ride with the windows open. Just in case I've still got germs or something. We're going to find more water.

Entry 7

It felt good to be riding in a car again. It might have even felt normal, except there were no other cars on the road. Jeremy insisted I ride in back with all the windows open in case I was contagious, but he agreed that there was probably something wrong with the water in that lake. No more drinking lake water, ever. Nancy and I played "I spy" while Jeremy drove. It was hard not to 'spy' bodies, burned-out cars, and looted stores. I did my best to pick mundane things.

It saddens me to think that the bodies and the wreckage of civilization won't mean the same to her. This is the world Nancy will grow up in. To me, it's sad and terrible. To her, this shit will all be normal. Rotting corpses in decaying cars crashed in the middle of the road will be as regular to her as breakfast.

We stopped at a little village in Southern Virginia. Jeremy showed me how to sterilize containers and get water from the water heaters of houses. It's incredible; most homes have thirty or forty gallons of potable water just hanging out. I feel a little silly. As an engineering student, I should have thought of that. Jeremy said it was because I never needed to before.

We also found a little .22 rifle in one house. We saw a lot of guns in this small town, but Jeremy said this one was just right for a beginner my size. He says he'll stay in this little village for a day or two to show me a few things, but he still wants to go to Washington.

I told him there's nothing there, and there's no way I'm going back, but the truth is I was so scared and lonely before that I'm thinking of going with them if they'll let me.

One good thing that happened is that Jeremy shot a deer. He made me help him butcher it. It was so disgusting, but he said I needed to know how to do it. I guess he's right. The food in the houses we found is going bad. It's hard to believe it hasn't even been that long since this all started.

Jeremy said an expert hunter would have done a much better job with the deer, but I guess we did ok. We had venison for dinner along with a few vegetables from the garden of the house next door. We also set up a rig to smoke and dry the deer meat for jerky.

We've seen a lot of deer and a ton of rabbits in this village. Jeremy says it's because the people are gone, so the animals are taking over.

The funniest thing that happened was that I found some beer when we were looking through the houses in the neighborhood for supplies. I had never tried beer before. A little wine at college, but that just made me feel like shit the next day. Jeremy had one with his venison, and I said I wanted one too.

I opened the can and took a big sip, then ran to the sink to spit it out. It was disgusting! It tasted like pee-flavored soda.

Jeremy and Nancy cracked up. Nancy laughed so hard the water she was drinking came out of her nose.

"Holy crap," I said, leaning over the sink, "how can you drink that stuff?"

"It's an acquired taste," Jeremy laughed.

"Why would you want to acquire it in the first place?" I spit in the sink again, trying to get the taste out of my mouth.

"I really don't know," he said.

Well, I guess that's all for now. I'll let you know how the shooting practice goes.

Entry 8

The last few days were bittersweet. Shooting practice went well. Gutting practice, on the other hand, was disgusting. I spent a day pretty much shooting targets off of a stone wall behind the house. I got pretty good too. Jeremy said I was a natural marksman. Markswoman or marksperson, I corrected him.

The next day, we spent hunting squirrels and rabbits. That didn't go so well. They're small and fast. I used up a lot of precious ammo. I did bag a squirrel and a rabbit, though, eventually, but then I had to gut them. I thought I was going to vomit. Especially when I gutted the squirrel. Apparently, I cut into the bowel. Frigging gross. Anyway, we ate a squirrel and rabbit for dinner. I didn't like the squirrel. It tasted like armpit. At least I have that skill set now.

The deer jerky we made came out pretty good. Now we have a bunch of it in case the hunting gets lean, or the ammo runs out. After dinner, Jeremy and I argued about going to Washington.

"You just walked out of the city on one road, at night. There could be Red Cross centers,

CDC, National Guard." He was getting kind of upset. "If there's anything still going on, it's in DC."

"There were no lights anywhere, no trucks, no signs, no bullhorns, nothing."

Jeremy folded his arms. "We're going." He wouldn't look at me.

"I'm not. I'm never going back there."

"You can't be out here on your own, Rachael."

"I made it just fine on my own before."

"You were dying when we found you."

I couldn't think of anything else to say. He was right. I wasn't going to say that, though.

The next day I went out and found a mountain bike. I got some saddle bags and stuff from the bike shop in the village. When I came back, Jeremy tried to help me put on the baskets I got on the bike.

I pushed him away. "I'm an engineering student."

"You were a *nuclear* engineering student. Are those radioactive baskets?"

I know he was trying to be funny, but honestly, I was kind of upset about saying goodbye to the only company I'd had in a long while.

When we were all packed up, I hugged Jeremy and Nancy. Nancy was crying.

I had to bite my lip not to cry too.

They drove north.

I watched until their black truck disappeared down the road. Then I pedaled south.

Entry 9

I rode south for two days after Jeremy and I split up. The clouds gave the air a chill, and the wind pushed against my efforts to pedal into it. As the day progressed, the wind grew stronger. In the afternoon, I started looking for a place to crash for the night. That's when it began to rain. I was riding south on the I-95. I figured I could make better time now that I had a bike. Still, I didn't see a moving car all day. No people. Total desolation.

As the sky darkened, I had to walk my bike because the wind blew so strong out of the southeast that I was getting nowhere riding into it. There weren't many abandoned cars, not like there are closer to the cities. The cars I did find all had bodies in them. The ones with closed windows look almost like mummies, all dried out from cooking in the summer sun and heat. The ones with open windows, well, you can smell them pretty far off, even if you have a clothespin on your nose (I keep one in my pocket now, just for that).

The wind picked up even more, driving the rain against my face so hard that it felt like I was being bitten by a cloud of mosquitoes.

The ditch that divides the highway started to fill up with water. Dark clouds made the night come early. I couldn't see anything. I was really getting scared.

The wind got even stronger, blowing me around a little. It blew the bike right out of my hands once. I could see some shapes ahead. Cars maybe. I was cold, soaked, and my jeans chafed my thighs. My feet started splashing in the rising water. At first, I thought it was just a puddle, but it kept going.

The shapes were cars! An unbroken line of cars. With this many cars, I figured there must be one with no bodies. I started checking with my flashlight. I hated to waste the batteries and lose my night vision, but the water on the highway was halfway up to my ankles. The water was rising fast, and I was worried. Would a car even be safe enough?

I saw a shape ahead, taller than the rest. It was a dump truck. I climbed up to the cab; the door was unlocked. I opened it. No bodies, no smell.

I unbuckled the crap from my bike and tossed it in. Then I stood in the wind and rain, trying to figure out what to do about my bike. It might blow away. I wished I had a bike lock. Isn't that funny? A bike lock when there's no one around to steal it. Anyway, there was no way to get the bike into the back of the dump truck; it was too tall. I ended up wedging it between the sets of back tires as best I could; then, I got in the truck.

I was so glad to be out of the storm. I started shivering. Funny, I wasn't shivering when I was out in the storm. I mean uncontrollable shaking. It wasn't even cold out. It's probably still August. I guess the wind and my soaked clothes made it worse. So, I stripped. The clothes in my saddlebags were mostly dry.

I have just about everything wrapped up in plastic bags. There were a few wet spots. I'm guessing the wind blew the rain under the flaps of my saddlebags. There must be a hole in the plastic bag with my clothes in it too. I made a mental note to check in the morning. Didn't really matter. Mostly dry is better than sopping wet.

Once I was in dry clothes, my shivering stopped, but I was still cold. I started looking around the truck to see if there was anything useful. There was! Keys! Way under the seat.

Maybe I could get some heat going if I could turn the truck on. I put the key in the ignition, trying not to get my hopes up. I've tried this before. Sometimes the dashboard lights come on, but there's just clicking under the hood. Sometimes the engine turns a few times, but the car never starts before the battery dies. Anyway, I turned the key two clicks, and the dashboard lights came on bright and strong. A good sign, right? I turned the key again. The engine turned, and the truck lurched forward, then the engine stopped. I almost cracked my head on the steering wheel.

Now it was a puzzle, something to keep my mind off the wind and rain outside. Leaves and small tree branches smacked against the windows. I focused on getting some heat. So, I figured if the truck moved when I turned the key, then it wasn't in park; it was in drive, except there was no park or drive. It had a stick shift. It took me a little while to figure it out. Lots of pushing on the extra pedal and wiggling the shifter.

When I finally got it, I started the truck, and in a little while: heat! The truck had plenty of gas in it, so I figured it would last the night. I laid my wet clothes on the seat, then started fiddling with the radio. I heard the most amazingly wonderful thing, and something terrible. I've got some problems to deal with right now, so I'll tell you about it next time.

Entry 10

So last time I told you about taking shelter from a severe storm in a dump truck. I picked up a broadcast from armed forces radio. I was so excited to learn that there were still armed forces!

Anyway, after I got over the excitement of hearing another voice, I settled in to listen. The announcer said that there were four survivor camps on the East Coast. There's one in South Carolina. I don't have a map, but I hope it's close. The radio said that each colony was on a military base. I'm not sure what to think about that. All I know about the military is what I've seen in the movies—and on film, they're not very nice. So that was the good news.

The bad news is that this isn't just a severe storm. They said that this was only the outer bands of Hurricane Jamie, an estimated category-four storm. They said that it was estimated because they didn't have the resources to check it. The hurricane was fifty miles off the coast, and they had no idea where or when it would make landfall. Terrific. They said the storm would affect parts of North and South Carolina for the next eighteen hours. I'm supposed to head away from the coast and seek high ground, but it's too late for that now.

I left the radio going, even though it was repeating a lot of the same stuff. It made me feel less alone. When the branches started flying into the windshield, I turned it up loud. Eventually, I fell asleep.

I woke up to a loud bang and the scraping of metal. The whole truck shook. My heart was pounding. By the time I was fully awake, the noise had stopped, just the rain, wind, and radio. I couldn't see anything through the windows, just the dashboard lights reflected in the rain on the glass. I couldn't go back to sleep.

I decided to try cracking the door open and shining my flashlight outside. Mistake! The wind blew against it so hard I had to wedge my foot in the door.

The wind and rain stung my face. I clicked on my flashlight and pointed it into the storm. The howling wind didn't drown out the sound of rushing water. The water was just a foot or so below the door. A strong current pushed sticks, leaves, and trash against the truck. When I aimed the light towards the back, I saw what banged into it and woke me up. The current pushed a little white car against the truck. It scared me a lot that the water was deep enough, and the current strong enough, to push cars around.

I didn't understand where so much water could come from... until dawn. It was a long couple of hours before gray light filtered through the storm. I was afraid the water would keep rising and drown me or sweep the truck away.

When it grew light enough, I could see the bridge ahead. Well, I couldn't see the bridge, actually. Instead, I saw a wave where the water swept over the place where the bridge should be. There were no cars in front of the truck, at least not anymore. In the side mirror, I saw where the current tapered away. The pavement was visible about ten car lengths behind me, but the water was too deep and the current too strong for me to risk getting out.

The water level outside the door was about the same as when I checked in the night. The announcer on the radio said that the eye wall was making landfall in North Carolina. At the speed the storm was moving, anyone in the eye would get about twenty minutes of clear weather. Maybe if the eye passes over me, I can see a way out of this. I don't want to chance staying in this truck for the second half of the storm. What if the river starts rising again? I can't see two of the cars that were behind the truck before.

I could try to swim for it, but the current looks pretty strong. I could try to back up, but I'm not sure I can make the stick shift work. Who would have thought that knowing how to drive a stick shift would be life or death? I guess if you don't hear from me, you'll know how it turns out.

Entry 11

I got it! I actually got the truck in reverse and backed out of the water! Probably should have tried that in the middle of the night instead of crying and listening to the radio. It took me half an hour of bucking and stalling, but I got it. It was kind of fun bashing into the cars behind me. I must have stalled the truck twenty times. It was getting hard to turn over at the end. I think I ran the battery down, starting it so much.

I was so glad to be safe, at least from the storm. After the eye wall passed, I spent the other half of the hurricane in the truck listening to the radio. There wasn't much new information, but just hearing a friendly voice brought a lot of comfort and courage. The wind let up around dusk, but the rain kept hammering down. I spent a second night sprawled out on that old bench seat.

In the morning, the clouds hung thick, gray, and low in the sky. A stiff breeze blew a chill into the August air. It kept raining off and on, but I felt like I needed to get going. My bike was gone, of course. I needed to find a map. When I set out on foot, the water was still roaring over the bridge, or at least where the bridge should be. I had no idea how to get across the river, or even if I needed to. I started walking toward where I thought east was, toward the coast. I figured I was on the I-95 southbound, so if I walked to the left, that should be east.

Then guess what? A helicopter went scream-ing overhead, heading for the coast too. You know, a compass would be convenient. Not that I know how to use one exactly, but at least it would tell me which way I was point-ing with the sun behind the clouds and all. I was so excited about the helicopter I started running after it. Stupid, I know. I didn't even have time to wave my hands or anything; it was going so fast. I had the saddlebags over my shoulder, and the damn thing slapped me in the boob with every step. I think I'm bruised there permanently. Finally, I slowed down to climb the fence bordering the highway, tossed my saddlebags over, and jumped after.

I did my best to follow the helicopter's trajec-tory. I crossed through this suburban neighbor-hood. The grass on all the lawns was thigh high. Leaves and branches covered the cars and the roads. There were trees and power lines down, but at least there was no electricity to worry about anymore. I had to retrace my steps quite a bit to avoid flooded streets. Hell, I don't even know if I'm headed the right way anymore. I kept my eye out for a gas station or any store that might have maps. I found one, but there were no maps there. Everyone used the maps on their phones, so I guess they stopped selling them. Sucks.

Tomorrow I'm going to have to start looking for houses I think nerds used to live in. Nerds like maps. That's dangerous work, though. Someone might still be home, and I don't want to get shot. My little .22 isn't going to get me out of much trouble if it comes to a gunfight. I'm not dumb enough to think shooting squirrels equals tactical training.

That was another thing. I saw lots of animals, especially deer. They're everywhere. Who would have thought they'd take over so fast? Anyway, I'm holed up for the night in a nice comfy van at a car dealership. The venison jerky is running low. I'm going to have to stop somewhere for a few days to hunt and make more unless I find some supplies soon. Holy shit! I just heard another helicopter fly over. I must be heading the right way. Maybe I'll find an army base or something tomorrow.

Entry 12

I can't think of a good reason to get up today. I just rode out a hurricane in an abandoned dump truck, alone. I mean, I could get up and keep walking east, or shoot a deer, gut it, and build a rig to smoke the meat, but why?

Before, there was always something to shoot for, you know, getting a summer internship at a nuclear power plant or an engineering firm, acing a nuclear isotopes paper, that kind of thing. But now, what's it for? What's the drive to survive? Shoot a deer so I can live long enough to shoot another one? It's bullshit, and I'm not doing it. What's the point?

I'm holed up in this little house. Nothing remarkable about it. Smells ok. I've got blankets and a small mattress laid out in the walk-in closet, so it stays warm. The light from the bedroom window is enough to read by. There's a little jerky left. The world is quiet. No more choppers.

You know when you lift something and have to hold it? Your arms start to shake. It starts to hurt. That's how I feel about the world. I'm supposed to be at my house with my brother, arguing about whose turn it is for dishes, not holed up in some fucking dead stranger's closet. I just can't do it anymore. At least, not today. So I'm not getting up.

I'm reading the books in this guy's house. There's a bunch about a guy who goes around helping people in trouble. He just does it because it's right, and kicks the bad guys' asses. I know it's fiction, but I don't think there ever was a guy like that. A guy who just helped people because it was the right thing to do. Everyone's out for themselves. That's how it was before, and it's got to be doubly like that now, except just about everyone is dead, and I'm alone. Always alone. I just don't see any reason to keep fighting.

Even if I manage to find a map and a survivor's colony, what then? There's no going back to school and getting good grades. No colleges. No jobs, except maybe farming my own food or something. No way. I just don't see the point in it. Will I find a man? Get married? Have kids? What would their lives be like? Constant struggle. Same as mine is now. I don't want to do that to a kid. Then what happens to me? I spend the rest of my life worrying about what's going to happen to that kid. How they're going to eat? Will there be a safe place for them to live? No thanks. Anyway, I'm not getting up. I'm tired of struggling and worrying. My arms are shaking and I'm going to drop everything. Just let it fall.

I'm going to lie here in this closet and read books and waste away. No one's going to cry. No one's going to miss me. No one will even notice. Someday someone will find me, and I'll be just another body stinking up just another house. There'll be no funeral, no mourners, no burial, just another rotting body thrown out onto the lawn to feed the flies and the worms.

Sorry, I'm just a sad sack today. Maybe I'll feel like getting up tomorrow, but today, if you even care, I'll be in this closet reading about a guy that could never exist. Just a woman no one knows exists reading about a guy who never did.

Entry 13

gave up. You know that. I told you that. I'm still lying here in this closet. I thought this would be the perfect place to call it quits. I'm out of food. Still have plenty of water, though. The water heater in this house was pretty full.

I'm getting too weak to carry the buckets of water upstairs to flush the toilet. I guess I haven't exactly chosen to die yet, because I'm worried about how it's going to smell up here after I can't carry the buckets anymore. I don't want to die in a stinking shithole.

Honestly, I'm not sure how long ago the food ran out. Two days? Three? I haven't been sleeping well. Every creak of this old house makes me jump. Is someone there? Is it a bad guy? The wind? A rat or raccoon?

I guess that's another way to tell that I haven't given up yet. Things still scare me. If things scare you, then you're afraid for your safety. Someone who wants to die wouldn't be scared of a rat or a bad guy, right?

So if that's true, then I guess I'd better get up and find some food, or it will make the choice of living or dying for me. The hunger cramps are pretty much gone. Now I'm just weak and tired.

I'm not sure if some of the sounds I'm hearing are real or not. I keep seeing things that aren't really there. Shadows mostly, as if someone walked by just before I looked. Do you think this house is haunted? I didn't find any bodies inside. Maybe it's an old ghost from before. I guess it doesn't matter. Since I've decided I'd rather hunt than die in this closet, I'm going to hunt.

Entry 14

I'm trying hard not to cry as I write this. I didn't have the strength to hunt. All I could do was to sit on the porch with my .22. I sat there all day. I saw a deer that I didn't have the strength to butcher or drag anywhere. All day I was cold. Even though it was warm and sunny, I had to wrap myself in a blanket.

A dog came by. I thought some company would be nice, so I called to him. Mistake! He was as hungry as I was, only I didn't look like company to him. I must have looked like Thanksgiving dinner.

As soon as he heard me call, he came charging at me, teeth bared. Didn't make a sound. So I...I'm crying again... I shot him. Twice, cause the first shot didn't drop him. He was a mutt with long reddish fur. I gutted him on the porch. I wasn't strong enough to carry him anywhere else to do it. What a fucking mess. I found a collar, blue, nylon, and faded. It had tags. He was someone's pet. Someone loved him once, just like me. The tags were too worn to read, thank God. I'm not sure I could have eaten him if I knew his name.

I built a fire on the front lawn from tree branches that came down in the hurricane and made a little spit for roasting his haunches. I choked it down, crying, then fell asleep in front of the fire. When I woke up, I cooked some more, then slept again. After the third time, I didn't trust the meat. The flies were pretty bad. They wouldn't let me sleep. I'm feeling better, but I still need more food before I can move on. Maybe one more night in the closet. I've got a book I want to finish. It's another one about a good guy drifter who helps people. Where the fuck was he when I needed him?

Entry 15

Well, I finished my book. The good guy won. Big surprise, right? Then I prowled the neighborhood, looking for food. The lawns were all knee high now. You couldn't see where you were stepping. I almost broke my ankle on a kid's bike buried in the tall grass. I picked it up, but it was too rusted to use.

Further along, the grass writhed under my foot. Then a head came out of the grass and lunged at me. I felt a bump on my shoe. I screamed and jumped back. The snake slithered away. I ran into the closest house and checked my foot. It was okay. The snake wasn't big enough to bite through my shoe; I guess.

The bright side is that I found two packs of spaghetti noodles and a pouch of soup mix in the cabinet. The soup is cream of mushroom, gross. Still, I kept it for an emergency. Like my mom used to say, beggars can't be choosers. The place smelled like rotten cabbage. I had to get out of there.

As I was leaving, I heard the choppers. I ran out of the house, but they were gone by the time I was outside. When they were gone, I heard a plane high overhead. It was the first plane I'd heard since before everything went to shit. It stayed around for a long time, circling closer and closer.

After it flew over and circled away, it started raining red plastic cards. I'm not kidding. Not a lot of them, just a dozen on the entire street. I picked one up. The printing on the card was kind of crappy and smudged and written in Spanish. The other side of the card was in English. It read:

DANGER!
RADIATION!
EVACUATE THIS AREA IMMEDIATELY!
Accident at Sea Ridge Nuclear Power Station!
Evacuate to the west of I-95.
This area is contaminated.
Cover as much of your body as possible.
Scrub thoroughly. Discard all personal items and clothing.
Take as little as possible out of this area.
Do not touch objects that have been on the ground.

I dropped the card. I had to pick it up off of the ground to read it. Assholes.

I thought of the spaghetti and soup in my backpack. At least I didn't have to choke down that soup. I couldn't remember how long I'd traveled following the choppers from the 95. Was I following them toward a nuclear disaster the whole time? Stupid. I still don't have a paper map, but at least I know which direction to go. Still, it would be nice to have one to find a main road and get out of here quickly instead of aiming at the sunset and running from the dawn.

I'm holed up in a basement for the night. Underground is the best place to be in a radiation zone. The earth provides a decent barrier. I wish I had a radio or something.

I walked all day, trying to decide if I should stop and eat the spaghetti. I haven't had anything to eat since... since the dog.

This is a tricky one. I'm still weak from hunger, but weakness and fatigue are also signs of radiation poisoning. I haven't noticed any metallic taste in my mouth or an abundance of dead wildlife. There's no telling how much radiation I'm getting or how close I am to the plant. I hate not knowing exactly what happened, though I have a guess.

Most nuclear power plants in the US can only function for a few days without a lot of human intervention. And in case I haven't mentioned it, there aren't a lot of humans around anymore. So it could be a clogged water intake, broken pipe, stuck valve, lack of backup cooling fuel, anything really, and BOOM!

The only thing I can do is move west as fast as I can. Maybe put another day behind me before I stop to eat and sleep. I'll get less radiation if I walk for a day first. Without knowing the details of the disaster, it's hard to know if the water from the water heaters is safe to drink. Or, if I'm even a survivable distance from the nearest radiation source.

I'm keeping the spaghetti. If I find food at the end of the day, I'll eat that instead. Maybe it will be less contaminated.

I also took a gallon of water from the water heater. Hopefully, the metal protected it from radiation. Although, it's in a plastic jug now.

Walking through these empty suburban streets, some still flooded from the hurricane, it's sad to think it's all contaminated. No one will ever be able to live here again. I feel fine, by the way, just a little hungry.

I'm cooking the spaghetti, after all. I'm tired. I'm going to sleep.

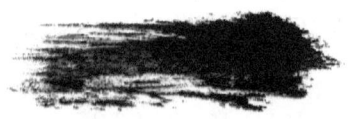

Entry 16

grabbed some canned food from the house I stayed in last night. The metal cans protect food a little better from radiation. I'm feeling a little stronger after a few days of eating. And I need the strength, too—canned food is heavy. But at least I have no signs of radiation sickness.

I stumbled onto a main road this morning, two lanes in either direction and a sign pointing west. The road isn't too plugged up with cars, either. I'm hoping other people got those red radiation warning cards. Maybe I can even catch a ride out of here. That got me thinking about people. I have no idea how long it's been since I spoke to another human being. I'm trying not to be sad. I would really like... no... I need to talk to someone, anyone, about anything.

The clear road got me thinking about the bike I lost in the hurricane. It would be a lot faster to pedal out of the radiation zone. Though the road is divided, there are still some houses along it here and there. So I started checking porches and garages. It was a tough choice because every step I took off of the road kept me in the radiation zone longer. But if I found a bike, I could make up that time and gain even more, so I looked.

In the afternoon, I was coming out of a garage—empty-handed—when I heard a squeaking sound and footsteps. FOOTSTEPS! I tiptoed around to the corner of the garage to look. It was a man walking west, pulling a wagon. There was a board on the wagon, and it looked like kids were lying on it. He was more staggering than walking, and he had a scarf wrapped around his head that covered his face.

I was torn. On the one hand, I wanted so desperately to talk to someone, anyone. On the other hand, anyone wrapped up in a scarf like that was bound to be trouble, but everyone in the world is bound to be trouble now. I decided to risk it.

I crept into the tall grass of the lawn and unslung the .22 from my back. As I crawled, all I could think about was stepping on that snake the other day, but I hiked up my big girl panties and got it done. Once I hid in the grass, gun pointed at him, I called out: "Hey you!"

He turned toward me but didn't see me. "What? Who? Who's there?" His voice was husky and raw sounding. He drew a pistol.

"Put the gun down. I won't hurt you."

"Okay." He bent down and put the gun on the pavement. "There. Please, help us."

"Help you with what?" I was starting to think this was a bad idea. The guy wasn't acting right. "Are you sick? Do you have the flu?"

"No... It's... I..." He mumbled something I couldn't hear.

"Speak up. What's wrong?"

"We were very close to the power plant when it blew up."

Blew up? Shit. I knew I was wasting time. I
had to get out of there. "What am I supposed
to do about it?"

"Please. My... my children... please."

I didn't know what to do. If they were close,
and chunks of core rained down anywhere near
them, they were goners. Hell, they were probably a big source of radiation themselves at that
point. But I'm not a monster, and these were
human beings in need of some help. "Okay," I
said, "I'm coming out. One sudden move, and
I'll fill you full of lead." Yeah, I know, movie
cliche, but I thought it sounded tough.

I stood up. The guy kept still. I stepped care-
fully. I didn't want to trip with the safety off.
Also, I didn't want to step on any snakes. As I
got closer, I could smell the rot.

"Please, let me take off my scarf. I can't
breathe."

"Okay. Slowly." It didn't make sense to me.
He'd been pulling a wagon with the damn thing
on.

He unwrapped the scarf. The gangrene
stench grew stronger. Tufts of hair floated away
on the breeze as the scarf came away. His head
was a swollen pumpkin, distorting his features.
Oozing sores stood out on his red cracked skin.
I glanced at the kids on the wagon. They looked
the same, if not worse. My stomach churned. I
recoiled and must have stepped back because
he said, "No, no, don't go. Please, help us."

"How?"

"We're dying. We're in so much pain." He
looked at the wagon. "My babies—" then he
let out a wail and started bawling, a big ugly
cry. One of the kids joined in. I'm not even sure
the other was alive. "My babies..." he managed
between sobs.

"Okay, okay, calm down," I said, although I
was anything but calm myself. I just wanted to

get the fuck away from there. "What do you want me to do about it?"

"They're suffering so badly, so much pain, dying so slowly...."

"What can I—"

"End it. I'm sorry to ask. I can't do it myself. I tried. Oh, God!" then he started crying again. The kid on the wagon was louder than ever. I couldn't tell if it was a boy or a girl. Their crimson skin cracked away in places, leaving bloody oozing flesh. Then the kid started to tremble violently.

"I don't understand." I mean, I did... but I didn't. Didn't want to.

"Shoot them. Please. I can't. I can't end their—"

"NO!" I ran. I can't talk about it anymore.

Entry 17

I don't know how long I ran, but the faces of that father and his children chased me the entire way. Their fissured, oozing faces haunted every stride. The kid shaking and moaning lying on the wagon. The whole scene replayed over and over in my mind.

When I was too tired to run, I jogged. Then I walked, then ran some more. By nightfall, I was just stumbling blindly ahead like a zombie. I had no map and no idea where I was. I knew only that I was heading west on the road out of the radiation zone. I dared not stop or touch anything. I was scared to lie down and sleep. So I walked through the night wondering how much radiation I'd been exposed to, how long I'd wallowed in that closet surrounded by self-pity and free neutrons punching holes in my cells. But it was useless to wonder because I knew nothing. I knew only walking, fleeing.

I got very hungry. Stopping to cook was out of the question. I was running low on water too, and soon my mouth refused to make saliva. At every turn, every new symptom increased my terror. Was this a normal physiological symptom... or the radiation announcing my impending doom?

I was too tired to go fast. Not that I had the strength, anyway. And, I couldn't see very well. There was only a quarter moon to light my path. I barely had time to avoid the tree branches and other debris in the road as it resolved out of the shadows in front of me.

I wasn't there. Not really. If it's possible to sleep and walk, that's what I was doing. Still, the faces of that man and those children came up at me from the depths of my mind, oozing sores on their cheeks, desperation in their eyes.

I came back to myself in the twilight. Dull shapes in the night formed into cars and road signs. I heard birds in the trees. Until that moment, I hadn't noticed how perfect the silence was. I tried to think of the last time I'd heard birds. I couldn't. Were there birds yesterday? The day before? I just didn't know. Were they dead from radiation, or did I just not notice that they were there?

I started looking in the occasional car I passed for one free of corpses. I wasn't even thinking about the smiling flu virus anymore, just a corpse-free environment off the ground to lie down.

I heard rushing water off to my left. Water rushed through the trees from a river overflowing its banks. It reminded me of the flooded river that blocked my path and sent me walking east in the first place. The chances that there were two big rivers so close together seemed pretty small. This had to be the same river. Was I getting closer to the highway?

My fatigue forgotten, I walked faster. With the first rays of the sun, I noticed signs that the road had been underwater recently. Trash, sticks, and debris formed a high water line on the roofs of cars. The pavement turned sandy, then muddy. Soon I was walking on the grass on the far side of the road to stay out of the mire.

In the distance, a bridge, or the remains of one, loomed out of the twilight. I climbed up the muddy bank of the underpass onto the road above. There was my dump truck, just a little way down. It didn't look like anyone had been in it since I left. I climbed in and turned the key. The engine started right up. The radio was playing the information channel I'd left it on. The announcer was listing off radio frequencies, none of which made much sense to me until he said: "Citizens' Band, that's CB channel nine. Anyone in need of help should contact the survivor colony at Fort Walters on those frequencies."

I looked up at the CB that hung from the ceiling of the truck. I'd wasted an hour on it the last time I was here and got only static for my trouble. Still, worth another try. I turned it to channel 9, pulled the microphone down, and clicked the button. "Hello? This is Rachael; I'm trying to talk to the colony at Fort Walters. Can you hear me?"

Silence.

As soon as I hung up the microphone, the radio squawked to life. "Rachael, Rachael, This is Fort Walters. Do you copy? Over."

"Oh, my God! Oh my God!" I was shouting in the truck. I grabbed the microphone. "This is Rachael. I hear you!" I held the microphone, squeezing it in my hand, willing it to make noise again, but it didn't. There was only silence.

I dropped the microphone and wound up to punch the dashboard. Then the radio crackled to life again.

"Rachael, I think you are holding the button down after you're done talking. You have to let go of the button so you can hear me answer you. Do you copy? Over."

"I copy," I said, then let go of the button.

"Rachael, this is Fort Walters. Let me know you are done talking by saying over at the end. Are you in a safe place? Are you healthy? Over."

"I feel okay. I came from the radiation zone. I got one of the red cards the plane dropped. I'm on I-ninety-five in a dump truck by a flooded river. The bridge is gone. Over."

"Okay, Rachael. Don't give any more information over the radio. I'm sending help. Over."

"Why not? What's your name? Over."

"Call me Radar."

"Why shouldn't I give information to you? Over."

"I might not be the only one listening. Over."

"Well, that's scary. Over." Great. I was finally talking to another human being, finally in touch with a survivor colony, a community, and now this?

"Don't worry, Rachael. You've survived this long. You must've had a guardian angel. Now you have two. Over."

What the hell was this guy talking about? "What do you mean? Over?"

"I'll tell you when I meet you. Just sit tight. Help is on the way. Over."

"Will you keep talking to me, Radar? Until help gets here?" I waited.

"Rachael, you forgot to say over. Yes, I'll talk to you. How far into the red zone were you? Over."

"The red zone? Over."

"How far east of I-ninety-five? Over."

I heard a noise. I saw a military truck in my rearview mirror. "Wow, Radar, you guys are fast. There's a truck coming. Over."

"Rachael, that's not us. Get out of there. Hide under the truck near the back where the smashed-up car is. Over."

"Wait. How do you know that? Over."

"GO, GO, GO! RACHAEL, GO NOW!"

Before Radar let go of the microphone, I heard another voice in the background say, "... vengeance one-one—" I didn't know what that meant, but I got the hell out of there.

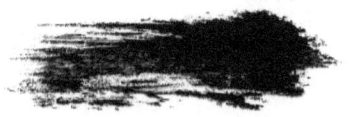

Entry 18

I scrambled out of the truck on the passenger's side so the people in the Humvee couldn't see me and crawled underneath. I went to the back and leaned against the car I'd backed into during the hurricane. How long ago was that? Anyway, I crouched there, trying to control my breathing. A truck pulled up somewhere nearby. A door slammed.

"Rachael, come on out. The guys on the radio are not the good guys. People that go with them never come back. They use people as slaves. A girl like you, well, you'll most likely end up a sex slave until you're pregnant. Then they'll just use you to make babies, chained up in some basement."

I shook with terror. Footsteps approached.

"Come on out, Rachael. Hurry, the bad guys are coming."

"I'm armed, and I don't trust you. Stay back," I said, trying to keep my voice steady.

"Are you going to trust some voice on the radio? Radar? Why wouldn't he tell you his real name? My name is Tom Anderson. I'm here to help you, but you have to hurry."

I couldn't think. My .22 shook in my hands. Should I trust this Tom Anderson or Radar, the voice on the radio?

"Come on, Rachael, we're running out of time."

Helicopter rotors split the air in the distance, getting closer.

"If you don't come out now, I can't help you."

Something in my mind clicked into gear. If this Anderson guy was a good guy, why didn't he ever cut in on the radio? Or warn me about the other guys? If he really was a good guy, he would have done that, right?

"Rachael, time's up."

I saw his feet by the tire. He bent down and looked at me. He looked just like a regular guy. The man was wearing a uniform. "Come on, sweetie, time to go."

I leveled the .22 at him. "I'm not going with you."

"Do you know what they'll do to you?"

The helicopter noise was getting louder. I felt maybe if I could stall this guy until the other guys got there, I might have a chance to figure this out. "I think you're talking about what you'll do to me."

"Come on!" His hand, which had been resting on the pavement, moved to his belt.

I flicked the safety on my .22. I couldn't remember if there was a round in the chamber. I couldn't remember the last time I fired it. I didn't want to chance ejecting an unused round and letting this guy know that I was scared and didn't know what I was doing, so I didn't work the bolt.

"You're not going to shoot me. You're just a scared kid." His hand came back into sight with a pistol. The other reached for me.

That pissed me off. Kid? Fuck him. Still, I wasn't ready to shoot him in the face right in front of me like that. I scooted out from under the truck on the other side. There was a guy there too. I ran. I heard the guy swear and start after me.

A shot rang out.

"The next one takes you down, honey," the guy chasing me called.

The helicopter was super loud now, right overhead. There were a lot of shots. I chanced a look back. The guy chasing me went down. Then there were even more shots. The helicopters (there were two now) were shooting machine guns at stuff behind me.

I got to the bridge, right to the edge of where it was washed away, and glanced over my shoulder. No one was chasing me. Bullets exploded all around the Humvee. I wondered if I'd made the right choice. Maybe the guys in the helicopters were the bad guys. I stared down at the raging river below. The missing piece of bridge jutted from the water's surface. Not a good place to jump.

The guns stopped. The helicopter noise got louder. I looked more closely at the choppers. One was fat; the other skinny. The skinny one was up high, circling. The fat one was coming down at the end of the bridge, cutting off my escape. I walked to the downstream side of the bridge and looked over at the water. I couldn't see anything, but I knew that didn't mean nothing was there. If I jumped, I might break my legs on something just below the surface or drown in the swift current.

I looked back at the helicopter at the end of the bridge. It hovered a few feet off the road. A soldier leaped out. I climbed the railing, ready to take my chances in the river.

The soldier ran toward me, screaming. I put one foot on the top railing. It took a few seconds for me to figure out what the soldier was saying because the helicopter was so loud.

"Rachael, wait!"

I waited.

She stopped running about ten feet away from me and held her hands up. "Don't, Rachael. I just want to talk."

"Then talk."

"Okay, will you come down off the railing?"

I shook my head.

"Rachael, I'm afraid you're going to fall. That water is moving very fast. There's lots of debris, and it's going to carry you into the radiation zone. Please come down." She moved closer.

"Okay," I said, "stop there then."

She did. I climbed down.

"Do you want to come to the survival colony?" she asked.

"How do I know the other guys weren't from the colony, and you're the bad guys? It's not like I can ask them. You shot them all."

"Well." She was silent for a moment, then said, "Wouldn't the bad guys make you go? Wouldn't they have guns on you? I just want to talk."

I looked at the helicopter hovering over the bridge. "You do have guns on me."

The woman said something into her radio, listened, then her body language said she was arguing with whoever was on the radio. Then the helicopter lifted up, moved down the road, and hovered over my dump truck.

"They can still shoot me from there," I said. It was easier to talk, but still loud.

"If they wanted to shoot you..." she trailed off, probably realizing the rest of that sentence didn't help her case.

I realized that, yeah, if they wanted to shoot me, they would have already. "Okay, so talk then."

"Okay, Rachael, I'm PFC Walker, United States Army, based out of Fort Walters, South Carolina, home of the Walterston Survivor Colony. I'm here to take you if you'd like to come."

"Those guys you killed said you'd make me a sex slave and chain me up in the basement."

"Well, that's what they'd do, probably. We know who they are, and we're working on stopping them." She looked at the chopper, then said something into her radio. "Rachael, we don't have much time. We're burning precious fuel for you."

"Why don't you kill the rest of those guys, like you did here? I bet that would be easy for you."

"Killing is never easy, nor should it be. The reason we don't is that there are innocent people with them. We want to rescue those people. We don't want them caught in the crossfire."

"Like me."

"Yeah. Rachael, we wanted to rescue you, too. I'm not going to lie. The world is fucked up right now. We've got to band together to unfuck it the best we can, and we need everyone's help. Everyone. Rachael, will you help us?"

"What can I do?"

"I don't know yet. We'll figure it out."

"What if I don't want to come?"

"I guess I'll give you what I can spare and directions to the colony in case you change your mind."

I liked that answer. It didn't seem like something the bad guys would say. "Okay, I'll go with you."

Entry 19

I got buckled down into the chopper in this weird tube chair. Three soldiers came running up from the direction of my old dump truck and jumped in. Then we took off at an angle that tipped me back in my seat. It was like riding a roller coaster backward. I must have looked sick because one of the guys elbowed another and grinned. The woman, who said her name was Walker, shouted: "Are you going to be sick?"

I shook my head. There was nothing in my stomach to throw up. I was shaking a little from all the adrenaline.

"Don't be scared, Rachael, it's going to be all right now," Walker shouted over the noise of the helicopter's engine.

I guess she thought I was shaking because I was scared. I wasn't, really. Something about her, about them, made me feel safe. It felt like things were back to the way they used to be before the flu. Funny, huh? Riding in an Army helicopter made me feel normal again. Maybe it was the sound of machines so long absent from my life, and such a fixture before the pandemic.

Once we leveled off, my stomach settled down, and the shaking stopped. No one spoke. Walker smiled at me, and I smiled back. I looked out the window, but all I could see was the sky. My eyes drooped. I must have run or walked for almost twenty-four hours.

"You okay?" Walker shouted.

I gave her a thumbs-up and closed my eyes. I woke up to someone shaking my knee. I grabbed for my .22, but it wasn't there.

"It's okay, it's okay, you're safe," Walker said, unbuckling me like a kid in a car seat. "We're here."

"Where?" I asked, trying to clear the fog from my brain.

"Fort Walters."

"The colony?" I asked.

"It's nearby. We're on base right now."

The engines were shutting down, and it was easier to hear her. I rubbed my eyes.

"How long since you slept?"

"Um... Where are we going?"

"You're going to the infirmary."

I didn't like that. I just, well, it sounds childish, but I didn't want Walker to leave me. Just her and the guys in the helicopter were more people than I'd seen in one place since the beginning, since before my brother died. "Will you come with me?"

"Sure, Rachael, I'll take you." She helped me out of the chopper and looked across the tarmac. "You're getting the VIP treatment! They've sent a car for you."

A beat-up old green car pulled up next to us. "VIP?" I said, looking at the shitbox.

"We are on strict fuel rationing standards. We walk everywhere. Fuel is reserved for missions."

We climbed into the car, and the driver sped off across the vast expanse of pavement toward a cluster of buildings at the other end. There were no planes moving, and I asked Walker about it.

"Well," she hesitated, "um, there are lots fewer people, not much fuel, so not many flights. It's as simple as that, really."

I could tell it wasn't quite as simple as that from her hesitation, but I decided to let it go for now. I had a lot of questions, but I didn't just want to call her Walker. "What's your name?"

"PFC—oh, uh, Cassie."

"Cassie, where will I stay?"

"Oh, I don't know, probably the infirmary tonight. Then if you're okay, maybe one of the dormitories."

"Dormitories? Like college? The ones at my school smelled like feet."

Cassie laughed. "They do sometimes, yes. Here we are."

The car stopped outside a squat brick building with a red cross above the double doors. It didn't look like much, but it was hard not to notice the lights—they were on! There was electricity here. I gawked at the lights and listened to Cassie's black boots squeak on the worn lime-green tile. She turned a corner and stopped at a desk there. She spoke to the man at the desk quietly so that I couldn't hear.

He peeked around her at me and gave me a friendly smile. "Come on over here, honey," he said.

I laughed. His swishy gayness was so out of place on an army base.

"What's so funny?" he asked in mock anger.

That only made it worse for me. The whole situation was so strange. He wasn't in fatigues, just scrubs. I tried to get myself under control to answer his question. "Well, I didn't expect to meet someone like you here."

"You mean you didn't think you'd meet a queen who could rock these baby-blue scrubs the way I do, surrounded by a sea of crew cuts and camo?"

"No," I said.

He held a dark hand to the corner of his mouth in a stage whisper. "Honey, neither did I, but a girl's gotta do what a girl's gotta do." He picked up a pen. "Now, have you been inoculated against the flu?"

"You have a vaccine?" I gasped.

"Yes, got it a week ago. Too late for a lot of people, but it's here now. So, I'm putting you down for a no on that. You must be naturally immune. Not many of us out there. Are you feeling okay? Anything wrong right now?"

"Well, I feel kind of weak and dizzy. I'm pretty hungry and thirsty."

He set the pen down. "When was the last time you had anything to eat or drink?"

I shrugged.

He looked at Cassie. "Didn't you give her anything?" He pointed to her canteen.

She looked at me, too. "Sorry, that was stupid of me."

"Okay, Rachael, come on back. Let's get you fixed up." He stood and opened the door beside the counter. "And you," he waved a finger at Cassie, "don't you have people to shoot or something?"

I still didn't want her to go. I felt kind of like I had a friend again. It was stupid, and I knew it. I looked down, embarrassed to meet her eye, to ask her to stay.

"I'll stop by later, okay, Rachael?"

I looked up and smiled. "Okay, thank you."

"Are you a doctor?" I asked the man in scrubs.

"No, honey, I'm more important than that. I'm a nurse." He held out his hand to me. "Lee

Stubs, but I'm thinking of having it changed."
He laughed. "Let's get you something to eat."
   He got me a glass of orange juice. ORANGE
JUICE! I didn't like it much before the world
ended, but now, OMG! I drank a second one
before he stopped me. He said I should take it
easy. I ate a breakfast MRE, which stands for
Meal Ready to Eat. To me, it was the best food
I had ever tasted. Lee said it was disgusting,
but I told him it was the first thing I'd eaten in
a long time that I didn't have to kill and skin
first. He didn't say anything to that, just stared
at me with his hand over his heart. He gave me
some vitamins, drew blood, and asked a million
questions about my medical history. Then, and
this is the best part, I got to take a long hot
shower. I think maybe he slipped something in
with the vitamins because I don't remember
anything else.

Entry 20

When I woke up in the Ft. Walters infir- mary on the second day, there was a note on the table beside me with a Hershey bar on it. It read:

Rachael,

Lee says you are doing just fine, but to let you sleep. I have the first part of the day free, so have Lee radio me and I'll show you around. Enjoy the chocolate.

Cassie

That was a great way to wake up. It felt good to have a friend again after all this time.

I got out of bed and found that Lee was off duty. The woman minding the clinic was a stern-faced, middle-aged redhead with a stab-wound mouth and a crisp camouflage attitude. She gave me a hard time about wanting coffee (not sure why) but relented and let me have a cup while we went over maps of the radiation zone to figure out ex- actly where I was and how much radiation I was exposed to. She didn't know herself. I guess it was some kind of secret because she took what we figured out and called it in to her boss.

I ate another awesome breakfast MRE, took another hot shower, and gave nurse no-lips about a pint each of blood, pee, and even some stool. Ugh. Cassie picked me up, and we rode bikes around the base. It was pretty boring until we got to the PX, which is a store that sells everything. Cassie bought me a pair of jeans for five chits (a chit is like a dollar), but the ice cream sandwich she bought was ten chits. I guess no one is making ice cream sandwiches anymore, and there are more jeans than asses, so those were cheap.

When I hugged Cassie for the jeans and the ice cream, I started crying. Totally embarrassing. I hadn't felt a hug since Jeremy and I parted ways; what? Weeks ago? It felt like much longer.

"Hey," Cassie whispered, "hey, it's all right."

I pulled away and hid my face. "Sorry. I... I'm really sorry. Maybe you should take me back to the clinic now." I was so embarrassed. I didn't want to look at her.

"Hey," I could tell she was trying to sound casual. "It's no big deal. You've been through a lot, don't worry about it."

But I did worry about it, all the way back to the infirmary.

When we got there, I was afraid to hug her goodbye, afraid I'd cry again. I didn't want her to go. I didn't want to be alone. I couldn't say that, of course. Cassie walked me in. Nurse no-lips had her panties in a wad because she had orders for me to report to building I, room 201, for testing.

"What, like radiation testing or something?" I asked.

"No. It was determined that, given your proximity and the duration of exposure, your radiation absorption doesn't warrant any treatment at this time. You are to report for aptitude testing."

"Aptitude testing? Aptitude for what?"

"That's what the test will determine," No-lips said. "Can you find it on your own?"

"I'll take her. I still have a little time before I go on duty," Cassie said.

We rode over to another featureless brick building, and Cassie came in to help me find the room.

The guy was kind of a dick, huffing and puffing about how he called the infirmary hours ago and how his time was too valuable to spend waiting for some kid.

Cassie clenched her fists and walked up to the desk. "Do you know what this *woman* was doing yesterday?"

The man just stared coldly at her.

"She was shooting and eating radioactive squirrels. That was before she got caught in a firefight between us and the Confederate National Guard. What were you doing? Sitting right here cleaning your fingernails, I bet." They stared at each other for a minute, then she just said, "Sir." and walked out of the room. "I'll find you later, Rachael," she called from the hallway.

Well, that didn't do anything to help Officer Dickhead's attitude while I was there taking the test. The test itself was like the college prep tests, but on steroids, with personality testing thrown in. It took hours. Officer Dickhead told me I'd be notified tomorrow about the results.

I asked him where I was supposed to go now, and he just sent me back to the infirmary. So I pedaled back there. Lee was on duty sitting at the counter.

"Hey girlfriend, I was wondering where you were. Cassie left a message for you. She said she arranged it so you could stay at her apartment, if you're okay with that."

"Oh, hell yeah!" I said. I sure wasn't looking forward to another night in the infirmary. I had to hang out until Cassie came to get me on her meal break. She pulled up in that same piece of shit that drove me to the infirmary on the first day. "Wow, the red carpet treatment," I said. "Why are you being so nice to me?"

She just looked straight ahead at the road. "Lots of reasons. I like you. There aren't many of us left, so, you know, everyone is special, and sistas got to stick together. And... you remind me of my sister."

I didn't know what to say to that. She looked like she was about to cry. I didn't have to guess what had happened to her sister. Same thing that happened to my brother, my mother, and seven billion other people.

The apartment was small, plain, and as close to heaven as I'd been in months. She had a DVD player and some DVDs.

I wonder what kind of job they'll give me?

Entry 21

I fell asleep watching DVDs. Cassie woke me when she got home at midnight, and we made pizza with some ingredients she'd stashed away. We did girl stuff, too. I won't bore you with all the details. Let's just say that I got a much-needed haircut and my own razor. I feel like a woman again!

In the morning, she brought me over to get the results of my aptitude test. The guy who met me wasn't the same dick that gave me the test. This guy smiled at me and gestured me into his office. "Hi, Rachael. I'm Major McShane. Would you like some coffee?"

"Yes, please," I said. What I thought was: suck on that nurse no-lips. After we both had our coffee in hand, McShane rubbed the ring of red hair around his bald head and gave me a doubtful look. "Now, Rachael, there are some things we need to go over before we talk about the results of your aptitude test. You state that your last grade completed was sophomore in college. Is that correct?"

I couldn't read his face, but something in his voice said that he didn't believe me. "Yes." I looked him in the eye.

He looked down at his paper. "And you state that you are nineteen years old. Is that correct as well?"

I didn't like the way this was going at all. "Are you calling me a liar, Major uh..." My indignation would have worked a lot better if I remembered his name.

"McShane, Major McShane, and no, I'm not calling you a liar. The test is."

What the hell was he talking about? "I don't understand."

"Your math and science scores were higher than many college graduates we tested. I need to verify you told the truth on the test form."

"I did." I crossed my arms over my chest. I didn't like where this was going.

"I believe you, Rachael, I do. That leaves only one explanation for your scores."

"I cheated?"

He smiled. "I doubt that. How could you? No, my explanation is that you are a most remarkable young woman. Based on your account of the last few months, I'd say a very tough young woman, too."

Well, I wasn't expecting that. "Um, thank you."

"You're welcome. More coffee?"

His unexpected compliments and, well, the whole situation, made me sort of nervous and jittery inside. "I'd better not."

"I shouldn't either," he said, refilling his cup from the carafe on the sideboard. He sat on the front edge of his desk right across from me, sipped his coffee, then said: "Rachael, I've been over your tests several times. I expected to give you options like farming or to put you on a resource-gathering team, but honestly, those would be a waste of what God gave you, Rachael."

"And what is that?" I asked, hoping he didn't mean something gross, like making babies.

"Brains, Rachael. I have something that will fit your natural aptitude for math and science to a T, but..."

"But what?"

"It's asking a lot. Please hear me out before you make up your mind."

"So whatever it is, I have a choice, then? I'm not drafted into the Army or something?"

"No, Rachael, there is no draft."

"So what's the deal?"

"Well, as you know, the flu wiped out over ninety-nine percent of the population. All services stopped. Everything stopped. The problem is that modern society just isn't that simple. There are many things that must be maintained—that can't just be stopped. Chemical plants that could explode—"

"And nuclear plants," I added.

"Exactly. Not to mention pipelines, oil rigs, trains full of poison, factories full of acid, and a thousand other things we are discovering every day. Rachael, if we don't work hard, all of us, this country will quickly become a toxic wasteland. If we hadn't dug in right away, it would already be too late."

"Dug in?" I asked.

"Early on in the pandemic, the President ordered the Chairman of the Joint Chiefs of Staff to create the Keeper Corps."

"Please tell me you aren't spelling corps with a K." Seriously. I hate that shit.

McShane shook his head. "In any case, the Keeper Corps was created. It's a joint military and civilian effort, and currently, it is woefully understaffed."

"And you want me to join?"

McShane smiled. "I'm prepared to beg."

"Why, what's the fuss about me?" It made no sense. "How am I valuable to something like that?"

"Well, Rachael, you are special. I don't want to overstate it. It's not like you are a super genius, but you are highly intelligent, with an aptitude for math and science. And you've got a couple of years of nuclear theory under your belt. Unfortunately, there are very few people left with those skills and abilities.

"There were over one hundred nuclear reactors operating when the pandemic—"

"You want me to work in a nuclear reactor? Yeah, I've got some knowledge of radioactive isotopes, but I don't know shit about the detailed workings of a pressurized water reactor."

"You know what? You're right. Let me just call Caltech and M.I.T." He put his hand next to his face with his pinky finger next to his mouth like a pretend telephone. "Hello? Yes? M.I.T.? I have a young woman here who needs a nuclear engineering degree... What? That's terrible." He pretended to hang up the phone. "Yeah, see, they're all dead."

"Okay, I get it. You don't have to be a dick about it." I didn't like being made fun of by someone who wanted my help.

"Sorry, Rachael. You see my point, though? There are so few people left alive, and of those, there are so few that have backgrounds in math and science. We have to train minds like yours with the aptitude for that kind of work, and we have to start right now! We have more than a hundred nuclear reactors that need looking after, and that's not even counting the military sites. They have their own fission to fry." He laughed at his own joke, then cleared his throat. "Anyway, these plants used to employ hundreds or even thousands of people, depending on the size of the plant. Of those people—"

"There are only a handful left alive for each plant, right?"

"That's right. You are a quick study. Of the people left alive, some have run off, and others might be electricians or pipefitters. Valuable and needed skills, but we need engineers and scientists very badly. We need to keep these plants safe."

"Why don't you just shut them down?" I asked.

"Rachael, they are shut down. They still have to be kept cool for up to ten years. The fuel is still hot."

"Then what?"

"We're working on it. Will you help us?"

"I don't think a couple of years of engineering education qualifies me for this."

"You will be apprenticed to someone in whatever position you're assigned. There is a Keeper Corps introduction meeting tomorrow. Go. See me afterward."

"Okay," I said.

Leaving McShane's office, I couldn't help thinking of everything that had happened since my last day of college. The pandemic. The news reports. My family and friends, dead and gone. My brother, of course. Then that man pulling his kids on the wagon.

An enormous lump formed in my throat as I stepped outside. But then, when the late summer sun hit my face, I thought of all the good things. The good people still working. Still trying to fix this mess and help the people still left alive. Jeremy and Nancy, and Cassie. McShane and the Keeper Corps. And right then, pedaling back to Cassie's apartment, I knew I wanted to be a part of it.

I know it sounds corny, but I want to make a difference. Help rebuild.
It starts with me.

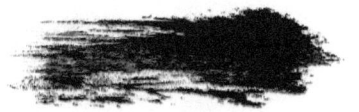

Part 2

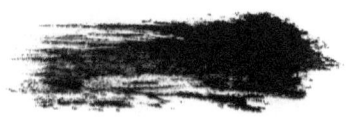

Entry 22

Well, I ran out of pages in my old diary, so I bought a new one at the Fort Walters PX. So here goes...

The glare of fluorescent lights made everyone look like smiling flu victims, all bluish, pale, and sickly. God only knows how I looked. I'd only been on base a few days. Before that, my only meals were irradiated spaghetti and barbecued dog.

Fifteen of us sat around tables arranged in a rectangle. There were a few old people, some middle-aged people, and me. No one was even close to my age. The fluorescent light in the corner flickered from time to time, which gave the whole thing a weird horror movie vibe.

The instructor was a musclebound crewcut in nerdy glasses and a shade of lipstick that screamed 'CLOWN!' She set some papers at the table by the chalkboard and looked us over. "Hi, I'm Sergeant Lindsay Schmidt. Welcome to the Keeper Corps. As you know, the flu wiped out over 99% of the population. All services stopped. Everything stopped. The problem is that modern society just isn't that simple. There are many things that must be maintained—that can't just be stopped. Chemical plants that could explode, nuclear power plants, pipelines, oil rigs, trains full of poison, factories full of acid, and a thousand other things we are discovering every day. That's why the Chairman of the Joint Chiefs created the Keeper Corps. We all have to do our parts. You're here because you possess special skills or aptitudes suitable for this kind of work. It's not just about the here and now. A thousand future generations are depending on the work we do today. Without our efforts, there will be no them."

Honestly, I felt like if she kept spouting lines like that, I might barf on my shoes. Who writes that shit?

"The Keeper Corps," Sergeant clown lipstick continued, "has three missions: One, public safety threat assessment. Two, public safety threat mitigation, and three, preservation in perpetuity of key assets and infrastructure.

"The job of the Keeper Corps is never done." She put up a map with the mid-Atlantic coast covered by a series of shaded squares. "Our unit, Whiskey Sierra Charlie, covers parts of South Carolina and Georgia, as you can see on the map in orange here." She pointed to the big orange square. "We have three categories of Public Safety Threats or PSTs. Level one is the most severe, and level three, the least.

"We are responsible for seventy-six level one sites. These include everything from nuclear power plants to chemical plants that manufactured methyl ethyl ketone and sulfuric acid to biological sites like CDC infectious disease research facilities."

I knew first-hand that the nuclear power plant she was talking about, Sea Ridge, had already blown up. Good luck cleaning up that mess.

"There are, as of right now," Sergeant lipstick went on, "two hundred and four level two sites. These consist of lesser chemical sites, pipelines, and fuel storage facilities.

"And, there are six thousand eight hundred and seventy-three level three sites that need to be secured or destroyed. These are literally everything else, from fertilizer factories to freight trains loaded with formaldehyde. Most level three sites will keep for years unless tampered with, which gives us time to take care of the more urgent problems.

"Those are the numbers we have now. The numbers we want you to remember: The estimated combined population of the Whiskey Sierra Charlie service area is about fifteen thousand people. Of those, an estimated ten thousand are simply out there somewhere, perhaps in their homes or on the road looking for help. One thousand are on farms, many started by the survivor colony. The rest are made up of the folks at the survivor colony itself, the Keeper Corps, and the military. For security reasons, I can't give you that breakdown."

That struck me as odd. Security reasons? Why would they withhold numbers? It made me think back to my conversation with Radar on the CB. He'd said, "I might not be the only one listening." After that, the guys in the Humvee tried to kidnap me. Cassie called them the Confederate National Guard, I think. So even though just about everyone is dead, there are still organized bad guys. And if the Keeper Corps is hiding its numbers... I raised my hand.

The instructor pointed at me. "Yes?"

"How dangerous is it to be in the Keeper Corps? Are groups like the Confederate National Guard trying to stop the Corps?"

Her big red lips frowned. "Well, it can be dangerous in the Keeper Corps, no doubt. But not nearly as dangerous as going it alone out there or doing nothing about these threats. If we do nothing, the eastern US will be a toxic wasteland by next summer, in some places much sooner.

In fact, Rachael, I believe you experienced this firsthand, didn't you?"

I nodded. I didn't like thinking about my time in the radiation zone. Starvation, depression, and the family with the burns, sores, and the smell of rot.

"There are great rewards," the instructor continued, "beyond saving the world. The biggest is food for life. As a member of the Keeper Corps, you will never have to worry about where your next meal is coming from."

"Are we talking about more MREs?" an old man in the corner asked.

"Sometimes," the instructor answered, "but more farms are coming online all the time. And if you haven't gone to the mess hall for fresh peaches in the last day or two, you're missing out."

The meeting went on for a long time after that. I'm not going to bore you with the rest. The short version is that along with food for life, you also get housing, probably on base, for a five-year commitment.

We apprentice with a professional as long as it takes to learn the job, whatever that job is, so we'll all be going into the field right away.

I can't say no. I feel a sense of duty. Also, I don't want any more red zones. I get my duty assignment by tomorrow. I guess they really are desperate to get people out in the field. The day after that, I'll be out saving the world. Pretty cool, huh?

Entry 23

This sucks. I can't believe I got dragged into all this saving-the-world crap. I'm stuck in... no *locked in* a nuclear power plant with a bunch of lecherous old guys, a middle-aged French woman named Sylvie, and four army guys.

At first, they had me sharing a room with Sylvie, but I've gotten used to being on my own. Also, she snores like a freight train. So, I cleared out a supply closet, and now I sleep there.

We all live in the control block of the Sea Ridge Nuclear Power Station along the corridor opposite the control room. They cleared out the administrative offices and bunked all the plant operators in them. We live in the reactor two complex. Reactor 1 is the one that blew up. As a result, we have to stay inside because of the radiation outside. Fluorescent lights and smelly old guys 24/7. Awesome.

Then there's the constant studying. I'm in the control room for ten hours a day. But I don't actually get to do anything. Just watch, ask questions, and do the bookwork Dr. Pearson gives me on boiling water reactors (BWRs), nuclear physics, etc. Then I get to go inspect the pipes and valves with Ron, a sweet old guy with Peter Rabbit teeth, and Phil, a cranky old bastard with a pot belly.

I thought I'd be saving the world. Instead, I'm a fucking plumber. I bet you are wondering how so few people are running a nuclear power plant, right? Well, we're not. See, the reactor is shut down. We just have to keep water flowing into the core and the spent fuel pool. We're not making power or modulating a controlled nuclear reaction (see, I have been studying). We're just trying to keep everything cool until it no longer needs water pumped in. Dr. Pearson says the reactor will be cool soon, but the spent fuel pool will need to be cooled for several years. There's two hundred tons of spent fuel in there. Job security, I guess.

The craziest thing I've learned so far though, is that a nuclear power plant has to have power. I know it sounds like an oxymoron, but it's true. If you shut down a reactor, everything is still hot, like stupid hot, so hot it will melt the nuclear fuel. That's what a meltdown is. It's literally the core melting and dripping down. Only it's so hot almost nothing can stop it. It just keeps going all the way to China. Well, not really, but you get the point. You have to keep the reactor cool. You have to keep pumping water in. You need power to run the pumps, and if the station isn't making any because the reactor is shut down, you need power from somewhere else.

Guess what? That's what happened at Three Mile Island, that's what happened at Fukushima, that's what happened at Chornobyl, and that's what happened right here at reactor 1. The start of those disasters was different in each case, but in the end, there wasn't enough water in the core to keep it from melting. And when the zirconium-clad uranium fuel bundles melt, they release hydrogen. And hydrogen explodes.

We're running on one of six diesel generators here. There are four backup generators and two emergency generators, which is stupid because, really, they're all backup generators. There's also a battery backup system if all that fails, but that will only keep things going for a few hours. Sorry to bore you with all this technical stuff, but I want you to understand what we're dealing with.

With all these safety systems and backups, you'd think the control room would look like Batman's cave, all computers and sleek modern controls, but no. It looks like a sixties spy movie threw up. All dials and knobs, and little lightbulbs instead of displays. Dr. Pearson says it's because lots of US nuclear power plants like this one were designed in the sixties and built in the seventies.

On my second day, I was near the top of the containment building with Ron and Phil inspecting pipes when the emergency klaxon started going off. That meant we had to get to a safety area outside the containment building. We were seven floors up and on the wrong side of the thick steel containment bulkheads. My vinyl booties slipped on the steel treads as I ran down the stairs. What a pain in the ass. My heart pounded, and my hands shook as they slid along the handrail. I didn't know what tripped the alarm. Was it something minor or an actual radiation leak? The radiation suit hood made it hard to breathe. I tripped on the stairs ripping the suit. My dosimeter, a little tag we have to wear that measures radiation, came off. As I lay face down at the edge of the metal landing, I watched the dosimeter tumble end over end into the darkness below.

I got up and rushed down the stairs toward the airlock. Ron and Phil's footfalls pounded on the stairs in between the blasts of the emergency klaxon. They were still way above me. When I got to the airlock, I still couldn't see either of them on the stairs. They are old and slow, so I knew it would take a minute for them to get there. They'd shown me how to work the containment airlock door to get to safety, but that would mean locking them in the reactor containment building until the airlock finished its cycle. If there was a big problem in there, those minutes might kill them, but their suits were intact. Mine was ripped. Blood ran down the yellow vinyl from my knee.

I wished I had a radio, but they didn't give me one. I looked up at the button to close the door, then over at the stairs. They'd come into view. They were waving their hands for me to wait.

Entry 24

When they finally reached me, we closed the inner door to the containment building and cycled through the outer blast door. Then, we kept on running to the emergency personnel bulkhead. Phil hit the big red button inside the heavy steel door, and it began to close. The whirring machines lent the odor of dust and ozone to the dank concrete chamber.

Ron called the control room to find out what was going on.

Phil helped me doff my suit.

I sat on the bench while Phil rummaged through the first aid kit. He came away with a scrub brush, so mean-looking the only thing I can compare it to is a toilet brush.

"You've got to be fucking kidding me?"

Phil grunted as he unceremoniously squirted some soapy shit on my leg and dug in with that evil brush. Hard. "Sorry, kid."

"I'm not a kid," I hissed through gritted teeth, refusing to acknowledge the moisture at the corners of my eyes. My leg screamed in fiery agony with each pass of the brush.

"Have to make sure there's no contamination."

"God damn it," I groaned.

Ron hung up the phone. "It's just a drill. Pearson said we were too slow. If there was a problem in the containment building, we'd be dead."

"That son of a bitch." Phil paused the brushing to stare at Ron. "That's bullshit. If the reactor was operating, maybe, but we wouldn't be in there if it were operating, would we? That bastard just wanted to make us run for it. Now Rachael is all banged up, with a torn suit and potential radiation exposure."

Exposed? I didn't like the sound of that.

"Don't worry, Rachael," Ron said, "I'm sure you're fine. Believe it or not, the containment building is pretty clean from a radiation perspective. Let's have a look at your dosimeter."

"It came off when I fell."

"Doesn't matter," Phil grunted, looking at his dosimeter, "we're well within tolerance. You didn't go anywhere we didn't go, did you?"

"No." I wiped my face with the back of my hand.

"You'll be fine," Ron said.

When the 'all-clear' sounded, we left the emergency bulkhead. Ron helped me hobble back to the control block. Then I threw up in the bathroom. I guess it was the stress and spent adrenaline. My hands shook for another half-hour.

When I felt better, I went into the control room to study. I glared at Dr. Pearson the whole time. After a while, he sat down next to me. His eyes were red, and stubble stood out on his face. He looked like shit.

"Rachael, I'm sorry you were scared, and I'm extra sorry you got hurt. Unfortunately, we have to conduct these drills. We have to stay on our toes." He looked across the control room at something I couldn't see.

I put my pen down on the half-life calculation worksheet. "Why? If the reactor is shut down, any emergency will take several hours to develop."

Pearson waved a hand. "Coolant flow and station power are just two emergency scenarios. It's true we can cope with those for a while. However, there is another kind of emergency: A hostile station takeover."

I hadn't really thought about that. "Why would anyone want to take over a shutdown power plant?"

"*Nuclear* power plant, Rachael, that is an important distinction. Anyone who took over this plant could hold half of the Eastern seaboard hostage. This place is as close as you can get to a nuclear bomb now."

That didn't make sense to me. Even if the plant blew up with an active core running at 100%, it wouldn't be anything like a nuclear bomb, not even close. "No. Even I know that."

"Well, it wouldn't be nearly as destructive as a nuclear bomb in the short term. The long-term effects would be much worse, though. But, more importantly, dirty bombs could be made from the spent fuel and placed anywhere."

"Who would do that? There are so few people left. Anyone can have just about anything they want. They can just go take it." This whole thing made no sense to me.

"Power, Rachael." He put his hand over mine.

I pulled mine away. Lecherous old bastard.

"Men seek power, both the kinetic kind this place provides and political. The man who controls this plant could make himself king of the Eastern United States."

There was a smile at the corner of his mouth and a faraway look in his eye that made me shiver...and wonder.

After my time in the control room, I limped down the hall to find Ron. He was doing pushups in the room he shared with Phil. I hid a smile. If anyone should be doing pushups, it was Phil, fat bastard, but Phil was watching something on his laptop with headphones in.

Ron looked up when he saw me come in. "Hi, Rachael," he grunted, "three hundred and fifty-three."

I laughed.

"After that drill today, I decided I need to get in shape. What's up?"

"Can I talk to you privately?" I asked.

Ron smiled and looked over at Phil. "He can't hear us. Watch this: Phil, Rachael found some Twinkies!"

Phil didn't even look at us.

"See? So, what's on your mind?" Phil's Ss whistled slightly through his buck teeth.

"What do you think of Dr. Pearson?"

Ron lowered his voice. "He's kind of a superior son-of-a-bitch. Smart though. Why?"

I told him about my conversation with Dr. Pearson.

"That's very interesting." He guided me into the hall. "He has been acting a little weird. Let's both keep an eye on him. If you see or hear anything else weird, come tell me. We'll keep this to ourselves for now. If he is up to something, he won't be alone. This place is too much for one man to handle. We don't know who we can trust."

"What about the military guards?" I asked, thinking of the team stationed at the plant.

"Like I said, if he's up to something, he won't be alone, and he'll definitely need them. If something is going on, at least one of them will be in on it too. Best to watch and listen for now."

"We have to tell someone!" I couldn't believe Ron was suggesting we keep this a secret.

"Tell them what? That he's a creepy douchebag? No, we need something to tell, and I don't know who we'd tell it to yet."

"Okay," I said. I didn't like it. I didn't want to just wait for something to happen.

Entry 25

The first part of last week I did my shifts in the control room, watching, studying, and asking questions. I also followed Ron and Phil around on their inspections.

The monotony of spending day after day locked in a building with no windows started to bear down on my soul. I felt the absence of sun and wind as strongly as I felt the itch from the scab on my knee from the reactor drill.

The Keeper Corps got me a laptop with a bunch of movies and music on it. I would have been more excited about it before, in my old life. But now...well, it just wasn't the same. It's hard to get interested in movies about college kid problems when colleges are gone. Most of the problems are gone too. I don't think I'll ever have to worry about what the captain of the football team thinks of me.

"Knock knock?"

I looked up to see Cassie leaning a wiry muscled shoulder on the frame of my open door. Her bright eyes shone with mischief...maybe more?

"Holy shit!" I squealed. I jumped up and wrapped my arms around her. "What are you doing here?"

"Temporary duty assignment," she said. "One of the other guards is sick and had to go back to Ft. Walters, so I'm here for a week."

"That's great," I said, "I'm supposed to go back there in a week too."

"Well, I'll do my best to match up my off time with yours so we can hang out. The C.O. here is a pretty good guy."

"That would be amazing!"

"Okay, well, just stopped in to say 'hi,' gotta get back to it."

"Will I see you later, Cassie?"

"Tomorrow. I've got a present for you." She grinned, then pushed off the door jam and walked down the hall.

The second day Cassie was at the plant, I was doing my time in the control room as usual. I got up to get some water from the cooler on the back wall. When I crossed behind Dr. Pearson, sitting behind one of the few computers in our stone age control room, I saw that he was looking at reactor restart procedures. He turned in his chair as I was passing, but I'm pretty sure I looked away in time. I got my water and went back to my studies as quick as I could. I wondered if I was just paranoid. Maybe Dr. Pearson had a perfectly legitimate reason for looking at startup procedures, but I couldn't think of one. Still, I had a lot to learn about the plant, a lifetime's worth, really.

In the afternoon, when I went on my inspections with Ron and Phil, I was dying to tell Ron what I'd seen, but Phil was always right there. Finally, when we were almost done, Phil went for a pee break, and I told Ron.

"Jesus," he breathed, "what can he be thinking? He can't start the reactor up with *this* crew. There's not enough knowledgeable people to run it. We can barely keep up with things as it is. Are you positive he was looking at startup? Could he have been looking at fuel removal procedures?"

"I know what I saw." I was sure. The heading was clear on the screen.

"Okay, let me think about this," Ron said. "I think you might be right. I think it might be time to tell someone about this. I'm just not sure who. In the meantime, keep an eye on Dr. Pearson, but keep your distance too."

I swallowed hard. "Ron, this is scary shit."

"I know. It'll be all right, don't worry. We'll handle it."

I was worried, though. What if Dr. Pearson was crazy enough to try firing up the reactor again? Why would he do that? It made no sense.

When I got back to my room, Cassie was waiting for me with a big grin and a box.

"What's up?" I asked.

"Open it." She gestured at the box.

I did. It was an Xbox! "Aww, that's awesome! Thanks, Cassie." I tried to be excited about it, but I was worried about all the shit going on at the plant.

"What is it? Don't you like video games? I know it's not the latest greatest, but...."

"No, Cassie, it's great, thank you. It's just...."

I closed the door and told her everything.

"I know you had the .22 rifle when we met. Do you think you'd be comfortable with a pistol?"

"Yes."

She reached down and pulled up the pant leg of her fatigues. There was a little automatic holstered to her calf. She unbuckled it and showed me how to strap it on. Then she showed me how to work the gun itself. "I hope you never need to use it."

"Don't you need it?" I asked.

"I've got another, it's not as small as that one, but it'll work. I'd feel better if you had that."

"Okay," I said. I have to admit, I felt better with the weight of it tugging at my calf.

"It's only a five-round magazine, so take time to aim. Make every shot count. Remember, if you get in trouble, don't just whip it out and start shooting. Wait for your moment. Got it?"

I nodded. It was a scary thought.

"Good. I'll tell my Sergeant about Dr. Pearson. In the meantime, you just act like everything is normal, okay?"

"I'll do my best. I'm not much of an actress."

"You'll do fine," she smiled. Our faces were only a few inches apart. Her minty breath washed over me.

Awkward.

I looked at her plump lips.

"Are you going to try it?"

All I could think about was kissing her. Yes, I'd like to—

"The game?" Her grin widened.

"Oh, yeah, let's check it out." I turned away so she couldn't see how flushed I was all of a sudden.

Entry 26

Things picked up steam after Cassie gave me the gun. The first thing that happened was that we got a special truck delivery. That's weird for two reasons: one is the truck delivery itself. Usually, the deliveries come in by chopper because of the radiation from the reactor one explosion. The second thing is what was delivered: grow lights, fertilizer, and some electronics.

The only reason I know what was in the shipment is that Ron skipped out on our daily plant inspections, and I was stuck with Phil's grumpy ass all afternoon. While we were walking around, I saw Ron moving a pallet of white sacks with a forklift. He set them down outside the electronics shop. When I asked about it later, he said they were doing an experiment to create power for hydroponics with spent fuel. What I didn't get was what they needed all that fertilizer for. I mean, there was one small box of grow lights and a whole pallet of fertilizer sacks.

My studies this week were focused on spent fuel from the nuclear reactor. When the fuel rods become inefficient at causing a nuclear reaction, they get transferred to the spent fuel pool. They have to be kept under thirty feet of water for up to ten years because they're still so hot, not to mention radioactive. The water cools them and provides a radiation shield.

That residual heat is called decay heat. The fuel rod assemblies in the spent fuel pool are in five groups based on when they came out of the reactor. Operating Cycle Phase 1 consists of fuel right out of the reactor, and OCP 5 is fuel that is almost cool enough to remove from the pool and store in thick steel casks.

Sorry if that sounded like a lecture, but the reason I told you is that when I did my control room time the day after we got the fertilizer delivery, Dr. Pearson kept having me check the temperature of the different OCP groups. The weird thing about that is: who cares? As long as the temp of the coolant in the spent fuel pool is around eighty degrees Fahrenheit, it doesn't matter what the temperature of the individual fuel groups are. Everything's cool, literally. Then I saw Ron rearranging the fuel assemblies on the crane at the spent fuel pool. I had no idea why the hell he might do that. I really needed to talk to him and Cassie.

I caught Dr. Pearson looking at plant powerup procedures on the computer again. I wished there was someone who knew about all this stuff that I could trust. There were a couple of other operators, but they were on different shifts. I thought maybe I could trust Sylvie, but I decided I should ask Cassie before expanding the circle.

After dinner, Cassie and I sat cross-legged on the floor, talking while we played video games. I don't even remember which one. I didn't want to tell her, but video games—not my thing. I told Cassie about my day and asked her if she thought I could trust Sylvie.

"I don't know, Rach, the fewer people who know that we think something is up, the better."

"Did you tell your commanding officer?" I asked.

"Yeah, don't worry, Rach, he's one of the good guys. We'll get it sorted out."

"I still really think I need to bring Sylvie in on this. I don't understand all this stuff yet, and she's an IAEA inspector. She knows."

"A what?" Cassie asked.

"An International Atomic Energy Agency Inspector. She got stuck here when they closed the borders during the epidemic."

"Are you sure we can trust her?" Cassie asked.

"No, but I have a good feeling about her."

"I don't like it, Rach," Cassie put down her controller and looked at me. "You'd be putting all our lives in the hands of someone you've only got a good feeling about. Maybe even the lives of folks for hundreds of miles around."

I hated this, all of it. I have always hated keeping secrets. "I wish your commanding officer told you what they were going to do about all of this weird shit. I'd feel a lot better if this place was swarming with army guys."

"Yeah, well, what about army chicks?" Cassie elbowed me in the ribs. "Seriously though, the army doesn't work that way. If you don't need to know, believe me, they aren't telling you. Don't worry, we'll handle it, and you'll be safely back at Ft. Walters."

"The hell I will!"

"Ssshh," Cassie hissed. "Boy, are you a shitty spy." She grinned. "The chopper for you to go back to The Fort comes in five days. I doubt the bad guys will do anything before that, and you will be on that chopper out of here. I want you safe."

There it was again, that unexpected softness in her eyes. I was suddenly aware of the warmth her twill-clad knee imparted to my thigh.

I nodded, but I had no intention of getting on that chopper. As much as I was sick of being stuck in this concrete prison, I was part of this. They needed me. I wanted to put all the pieces of this weird puzzle together.

It occurred to me that I hadn't discussed the strange truck shipment with Cassie, so I asked her about it.

"I wasn't on duty when it came in. Just getting a truck shipment is weird, though, from what I hear. What came in that they'd risk sending a truck through the red zone?"

"Some electronics, a box of grow lights, and a pallet of fertilizer sacks," I said. "The thing I can't figure out is, what they need all that fertilizer for if there's just one box of grow lights."

She gave me a strange look. "What kind of fertilizer?"

"Ammonium something."

"Ammonium nitrate?"

"That sounds right," I said. "What would they need all that for?"

"A bomb."

Entry 27

I couldn't believe what Cassie said about the fertilizer being used for a bomb. "Why would they make a bomb? This whole place could be turned into a bomb without a big load of fertilizer."

"I don't know Rach, but we have to find out," Cassie said. "Then you're on the next chopper out of here."

"I'm not leaving," I said. Part of it was wanting to solve the mystery of the ammonium nitrate fertilizer. Part of it was that I didn't want to be separated from Cassie. Our only contact, her knee on my thigh as we sat cross-legged on the floor of my supply closet turned bedroom, playing video games. I wanted her to reach out and take my hand. Take me into her arms.

"I care about you, Rach—"

My heart leapt into my throat.

"—so I'm going to make sure you are on that chopper in five days."

Not what I wanted her next words to be.

I'll let my Commanding Officer know what's going on." She put her arm around me and squeezed my shoulder. "Cool?"

Oh, it was cool, but not the thing she was talking about. The strength of her fingers bolstered my confidence. I rested my head on her shoulder. "Cooool."

"Good. You just keep playing it cool, and we'll get this figured out and fixed up."

Playing it cool. Right. I lifted my head and pulled away from her embrace.

That night, between thoughts about Cassie, I stared into the darkness trying to put the pieces together in my mind. There was fertilizer—a bomb maybe—and Dr. Pearson's speech about hostile plant takeovers. Ron working on the hydroponics project, Ron rearranging spent nuclear fuel in the spent fuel pool, which, I had to admit, might have a perfectly logical explanation. I really needed to talk to Sylvie. Out of all the others that rotated through the control room, she was the only one who called people on their bullshit.

It turned out I didn't have to find an opportunity to talk to Sylvie; she came to find me. I'd just had breakfast and was brushing my teeth in the ladies' room when she came in.

"Rachael," she said.

I adore her accent by the way.

Her hazel eyes shone intensely from under her strawberry bangs. "Can we speak privately?"

"Aren't we?" I asked through a mouth full of toothpaste.

"More zan this," she said.

"Okay, come back to my room with me."

"Rachael," she whispered when the door was closed. "I know you are new at zis, but I want to ask if you have seen somezing strange lately."

I didn't know whether to trust her at that moment. True, I'd been planning to talk to her, but her asking me like this, I wondered if Dr. Pearson had put her up to it to find out if people suspected anything. I hesitated.

"Thought so," she said. I guess my expression gave me away. "Ron's been rearranging the spent fuel in the pool."

"I noticed," I sat down on my cot. "I figured he had a good reason."

"There are no good reasons, only bad ones," she breathed.

"Like what?"

"After 9/11 the Nuclear Regulatory Commission ordered all US plants to distribute spent fuel evenly throughout the pool so that terrorists couldn't easily blow up the hot fuel or steal the cool fuel. Ron is undoing that. He's gathering all the fuel groups together. The only reason for that, is to either blow it up or steal it."

"You think he's trying to steal it?" I asked.

"If so, he is stupid. Everyzhing in zat pool is too hot to put in a dry cask. It would melt, zhen explode."

"Explode? Like a nuclear bomb? I thought spent fuel wasn't radioactive enough?"

"Not like a nuclear bomb. A dirty bomb. When fuel bundles melt zhey release hydrogen."

"What if they were also packed with explosives?" I asked.

"What are you talking about?"

I told her about the hundred sacks of ammonium nitrate.

"Sacre bleu! Zis would make a very large dirty bomb. Zere are two hundred tonnes of spent fuel in that pool. Perhaps ze ammonium nitrate is enough to cause a chain reaction."

"Like a nuclear bomb?" I asked.

"Zat kind of math is too much for me, but it is possible. We must tell someone!"

"I have, and I'll pass this new information along. The question is: when are they planning on doing this?"

"I would say zat they will do something while most of us are away next week. Most of ze staff will be off-site."

That information definitely made me rethink my plan to hide out and stop Dr. Pearson.

After my talk with Sylvie, I had to face the fact that Ron, that old buck toothed power plant worker I'd been helping with the inspections, was part of whatever was going on. The fertilizer should have been a big clue for me, but he was so friendly. Thinking back, he did try to imply that Phil was the one that was suspect. Did that mean that Phil wasn't in on it?

My problem now was that I had to go four more days pretending that I didn't know something was up. Four more days to figure things out. Let's just hope I can pull this off.

Entry 28

I had to think long and hard about my plan to stay at the power plant, considering someone was building a nuclear bomb, well, possibly building a nuclear bomb, we didn't know for sure, the only one who could do the math was Dr. Pearson, and he was the one behind the whole thing.

Then there was the Cassie situation. I hadn't seen her since the day before. I didn't want to leave her. And I couldn't imagine sitting back at Ft. Walters wondering what was going on...if she was safe.

Even though I hadn't decided whether to stay or not, I did decide if I was going to be sneaking around avoiding surveillance cameras for a few days I might get hungry, so I started stashing MREs (that's Meals Ready to Eat, in case you forgot) in secret little spots around the plant where I thought I might hide. It wasn't that hard really. I always carried a tool bag on afternoon inspections, a couple of MREs didn't make it any heavier really.

The hard part, at least for me, was acting like everything was cool around Ron, Phil, and Dr. Pearson. I did my best, but I was so worried I was going to blow it, that I ended up pretending to be sick and hanging out in my room for a day. I felt like shit about it. I wasn't doing any good in my room. I just sat there wondering about what was going on out in the plant. Cassie and Sylvie both checked in on me, then kicked me in the ass to get back out there.

I ended up getting up and going on my afternoon inspections. When we got to the electronics workroom, Ron dropped out of inspections. He said he had things to do to get ready to transfer the spent fuel to dry casks. That made Phil, who was usually grumpy, even grumpier.

"Son of a bitch is just playing hooky," Phil mumbled. "Transferring the spent fuel has nothing to do with anything he could be doing in the electronics shop. There's more here to inspect than the two of us could do right in a week, never mind an afternoon. That guy is an asshole." Phil spat between a set of thick high-pressure pipes that ran floor to ceiling. "See that wet spot?" He pointed to the spittle on the concrete. "If I didn't spit in front of you, you'd never notice that little dark spot on the concrete between the pipes. If that came from one of these pipe joints, it wouldn't be enough to trip the pressure sensors, but these are high-pressure pipes, part of the hot leg of the primary cooling system. By the time that leak was big enough to register in the control room, this whole area would be contaminated." Phil grunted, and he climbed the metal steps in front of me, heading deeper into the containment building.

"It's like he doesn't care if this thing is maintained. He's not thinking past next week. He just wants to fiddle with his hydroponics and play solitaire with the spent fuel in the pool."

All this time I assumed Phil was in on whatever Ron and Dr. Pearson were up to, but now hearing him talk, I wondered if he might just be a grumpy ally. I decided to try bringing Phil into the group with Cassie, Sylvie, and me. So I threw out a few breadcrumbs to see how he reacted. "It's total bullshit, what Ron's doing I mean. They have a whole pallet of fertilizer for one box of grow lights."

Phil snorted. "That doesn't even scratch the surface of the bullshit that's happening here. All this shit about transferring fuel to dry casks. It's ridiculous. There aren't enough casks available to store what's in the pool. Two hundred tons! Did you know that? The original Keeper Corps plan was to get all the spent fuel assemblies to OCP5 status, then cover the whole mess in sand and cap it in concrete. I don't even understand why all of a sudden we're fucking with dry cask storage."

"I don't either," I said.

He gave me a wry look. "Kid, of course you don't. You just got here. You just started learning about all this shit. I mean, what do you know about it?"

I did my best to keep my cool and not let this asshole get to me. Asshole or not, he seemed to be one of the good guys. "I know that OCP5 stands for Operating Cycle Phase. I know that OCP5 is the coolest of the five phases of fuel, and the only one that can be safely put in dry storage. I know Ron is breaking the law by lining up the fuel rods by their OCP. I know he's lining up hot fuel near the cask loading area."

"He's planning on loading hot fuel into the casks? That's nuts. It won't hold. Are you sure? How do you know?"

"Well, the fuel handling crane was updated since the plant was built; it actually has computer control. The system logs every crane move. Seems like Ron doesn't know, or doesn't care."

Phil looked at me in wonder. "Well kid, I guess I was wrong. I guess you do know something."

I tried to hide my smile, hide how good his words made me feel. "Phil, what do you think is really going on around here?" I asked, curious to see if he would reveal himself to be one of the good guys.

"I don't know, Rachael, all I know is, I'm looking forward to getting on that chopper in three days. Especially if Ron is going to try to load hot fuel into the casks. It won't hold."

"It won't?"

"No. It will melt the casks."

I felt a pit forming in my stomach. "How long would that take?"

"Don't know," he said, "few hours or a few days, depending."

"Depending on what?"

"Whether he pumps the water and air out of the casks and fills them with helium or CO_2, the ambient temperature of the spent fuel, lots of variables."

"What would anyone want with hot spent fuel?"

"I can only think of one thing," he said.

"A bomb?" I asked.

"A bomb," he agreed.

Entry 29

Cassie's rich brown irises stared back at me as I passed on all the information I got from cranky old Ron about spent fuel being hot enough to melt the storage casks. Was there the same pent-up longing in her eyes I hid behind mine? Or was that some kind of wishful thinking? I wanted to kiss her. Throw myself in her arms. But no. This wasn't the time. There was too much shit going on around the plant for me to throw my hormones into the mix. Maybe after all this was over....

As the shit gets deeper around here, I am more and more glad that I have Cassie's little gun strapped to my ankle. It's so hard to walk around here not knowing who the good guys and bad guys are. At first, I thought Ron (remember the buck-toothed nice guy?) was one of the good guys because he was so nice to me, and Phil (the grumpy potbellied guy) was on the other side because of how mean he was. Now I realize that you just can't tell that way. I still haven't let Phil in on everything. Cassie says the fewer people who know, the better, at least for now.

There is only one more day left before the chopper comes, and I'm still not sure if I'm going to get on it. On the one hand, I'm in this so deep I feel like I should be here to help. On the other hand, we only have some pieces of the puzzle, and with only a couple of days to go, I have no idea how they fit together. Obviously, someone is making at least one bomb, maybe two; one with the ammonium nitrate outside the electronics shop, and possibly another with hot spent nuclear fuel loaded into dry storage casks. I still have no idea why.

Speaking of shit no one understands yet, I caught Dr. Pearson looking at reactor startup procedures again. He must think I'm either blind, stupid, or both. I mean, he was looking on the control room computer right in the middle of the day shift. I was starting to wonder if he wanted to be caught, like a serial killer leaving a calling card.

I told Phil about it when we were doing inspections of the spent fuel pool secondary feedwater system.

"That's ridiculous," he muttered as he held a telescoping mirror up to the underside of a pipe to examine the joint. "The core is almost in a cold shutdown state. Why would he start it back up again?"

"Cold shutdown?" I asked.

"Come on, Rachael; you should know this by now. When the core is cool enough that you no longer need to run the cooling pumps to keep it from melting, it's in cold shutdown."

"Oh, right." I felt stupid. I did know that, but I was focused on this startup thing and wasn't thinking clearly. "Ignoring that, if Dr. Pearson wanted to start up the plant again, could he?"

Phil collapsed the telescoping mirror between his hands and looked at me. "You've been studying, you tell me."

"I don't think so, not the right way."

"Because..." Phil prompted.

"Because there will be a skeleton crew here, not enough people."

"Yes." Phil nodded. "Even if the plant were staffed to normal Keeper Corps standards, it would take fifty more people to restart the nuclear reaction safely. You need to inspect all the systems. Not only that but it takes at least a week to go from a cold start to a normal operating temperature."

"A week?" that seemed like a long time to me. "I thought you just raised the control rods and started the cooling pumps."

Phil banged his fist on the pipe he'd just inspected. "This pipe has a two-inch wall thickness. The outside of the pipe is at room temperature, and the inside is heated to operating temperature too quickly, the temperature differential will make the metal crack. That obviously would be very bad. The solution is, you warm it a little and wait for the heat to sink all the way through the wall of the pipe, then you heat it a little more."

That set the gears in my mind turning. Of course, you couldn't just start back up. Dr. Pearson had to know that. "So there's no way to start it safely with a skeleton crew?"

"No," Phil said picking up his bag.

"What about unsafely?"

He turned to look at me. "What do you mean?"

"What if someone wanted to sabotage the plant? Could they restart the reactor?"

Phil thought about it for a minute. "I don't know much about the control side of operations. I guess if you knew how to bypass the safety systems it might be possible. You'd have to know the plant like the back of your hand;

how each system worked, all that. The only one here who knows the systems that well is—"

"Dr. Pearson," I finished for him.

"Do you seriously think Dr. Pearson is trying to sabotage this plant? He could have done that a long time ago if he wanted." Phil said. "He's been at the front line of trying to save what's left of this place from melting down or blowing up. It makes no sense."

"It might if he decided he wanted something more than being a power plant manager."

"Like what?" Phil asked.

I thought about what Cassie said about the fewer people who knew, the better, and I backpedaled. "I don't know."

I spent the rest of the day thinking about it. Pearson couldn't safely restart the reactor, but he was looking at the procedures, and he was doing it openly. Maybe there was some legitimate reason he was looking at them that I just don't understand yet. After all, I'm still a newbie. I'm going to talk with Sylvie and Cassie again. We have one more day before the choppers come to figure it out.

Entry 30

The day before the choppers were supposed to take me away from the plant came and went. I talked to Cassie and Sylvie a lot. I even talked to Phil about the situation with the ammonium nitrate and the spent fuel. In the end, none of us could figure out what was going on: the ruse about restarting the reactor, the ammonium nitrate, rearranging the spent fuel rods, none of it.

"You're getting on that chopper tomorrow, Rachael," Cassie said. She stood leaning on the metal doorframe of my storage closet turned bedroom. Her eyes bored into mine.

"Of course. I'm not staying here to get nuked or blown up." I turned away on the pretext of stuffing some clothes in my backpack.

"Look at me and say that," Cassie said sternly.

I looked into her eyes, "I'm getting on the chopper."

"Wow, are you a bad liar?"

"Cassie-"

"No, Rachael, leave this to the military."

"Cassie, you need someone who knows how this stuff works."

"You've been here less than a month Rachael, suddenly you're an expert on nuclear power plants?"

"I know more than you."

"Rachael, not everyone here will be in on it. Let us sort it out."

"I need to be here," I said angrily jamming a sweatshirt into my pack.

"And I need you gone. I—"

Say it, Cassie. Tell me.

She didn't.

Finally, I said, "I've got your gun..."

"Which you've never trained with. Hell, never even fired."

"Uggghhh!" I shoved a T-shirt into my bag.

"I will have a guard escort you to the chopper if I have to," she said through gritted teeth.

"Okay, okay, I'll go," I said, though I had no intention of going.

"I don't believe you."

"Whatever." I pulled the zipper on my pack so hard it broke.

I held up the zipper pull.

Cassie's stifled a laugh. "What are you so mad about anyway?"

"Don't you know?"

"Don't you think that question is a bit cliché?"

"Don't play dumb, Cassie. Because of how you feel about me?"

"Because of how I fe—oh, Rach, no. I—"

I wanted to die. No. I wanted to run, then I wanted to die. In a deep deep hole.

"Rach, you're like my little—"

"Don't say it."

"—sister," she finished.

"Could you give me some space? I have to finish packing."

"But you just finished packing. You broke the zip—"

"Could you give me some space?"

"Ok."

The next day Cassie made sure I had no way to escape the chopper line. She picked me up at my room and 'escorted' me down to the tarmac. We waited just inside the doors and watched on the security camera as a big twin-rotor helicopter touched down in the parking lot. A soldier in a bulky camouflage radiation suit hosed down the area around the chopper, just in case the wind from the rotors blew radioactive particles from the reactor 1 explosion onto the parking lot. I'd seen all this before. No big deal.

What happened next though was something new. The soldier who'd cleaned the parking lot approached the security camera with something on the end of a pole, then the camera went black.

Cassie and I looked at each other. A few seconds later a dozen soldiers came through the door.

"Of course," Cassie said, "they don't want anyone to know they're here."

Made sense to me.

Cassie had to lead the new guys to- well I don't know where they were going. "Get on the fucking chopper, Rachael," she called over her shoulder as she led them away.

"Yes, sir," I saluted. As we filed out to the chopper, I realized that Sylvie wasn't in line. I wasn't going to miss this, no way. I wanted to know what was going on—and help stop it.

Workers were unloading pallets of supplies and lining them up to go into the plant. I stopped to tie my shoe, then ducked behind a pallet of bottled water. I only had to wait a minute or two for the chopper to lift off, then I ran back to the door.

"Rachael, what the—" someone called behind me.

I didn't look back. I opened the door and ducked inside.

"I fucking knew it, you little shit!" Cassie stood just inside the door.

"Cassie, I—"

"Spare me, okay? Now you're going to stay right on my ass 'til this is over."

"Kinky," I did my best disarming smile.

"Shut up, Rach, I'm pissed at you. Come on."

She led me down to the security offices at the bottom of the control block. I'd never been down there before. It smelled like old feet. She banged on a locked steel door.

"Shit," a voice said through the door.

"Show," Cassie answered. The door opened.

Inside two men stared at a semicircular array of screens that took up half of the tiny room.

"What took you so long?" the closest man asked. He had skin as smooth and black as the keys on a piano, and when he spoke his teeth showed faintly blue in the light from the monitors.

"Sorry, Sergeant. She was cautious. She actually waited for the chopper to lift off," Cassie grinned.

"What?" I was totally confused. It sounded like they expected me.

"It was Sergeant Holmes's idea. He thought you'd be useful here, helping to interpret what we see on the cameras, especially the control room feed," Cassie said.

"How..."

"I have..." Holmes looked down, "had, two teenage daughters. The easiest way to get them to do something was to tell them they couldn't."

"Son of a bitch. You played me."

Sergeant Holmes grinned. "Yup."

"This is Lt. Clark," Holmes indicated the tall, thin, silent man looking on with his hands behind his back.

"Hello, Rachael. Now that everyone's had their fun, shall we buckle down and prevent a nuclear disaster? Hmmm?" Clark's eyes never left the screens.

Sergeant Holmes showed me how to move the cameras and zoom in on things. We sat there for hours, checking gauges in the control room. Then peering into the twilight on the external cameras.

The emergency klaxon sounded.

Entry 31

"Does anyone see any cause for the alarm?" Lt. Clark asked.

"I see some flashing lights in the control room," I said, "but it's going to take me a few minutes to zoom the cameras in on each one and find out what's happening."

"Sergeant Holmes, call the control room, see what's going on," the Lt. said.

I heard Holmes talking to somewhere behind me. I frantically zoomed the camera around the control room from flashing light to flashing light. I saw low core water level indicators, feedwater pressure indicators, and pump rpm warning indicators.

"Dr. Pearson says there's a feedwater power supply problem," Holmes said.

I zoomed in on the big black handles that controlled the pumps. Instead of straight up and down, which was the automatic position, they were turned to the left, the off position. Pearson or someone, manually shut off the pumps that were keeping the reactor cool. "Oh, there's a power supply problem all right," I said. "The power has been turned off. The pumps have been manually disabled from the control room."

"The computer let them do that?" Cassie breathed.

"What computer?" I zoomed in on the switches as much as I could. "My smartphone has more computing power—"

"—than a nuclear power plant?" Sergeant Holmes was incredulous.

"More than this one anyway. It was designed in the sixties, built in the seventies."

"Our tech down here says the switches are in the off position," Sergeant Holmes said into the phone.

On my security screen I saw Dr. Pearson look into the camera, then nodded and spoke into the phone.

Sgt. Holmes listened, then held the receiver to his chest so Dr. Pearson couldn't hear. "He says they're being serviced, and that there is no danger. They will be operational before the core gets too hot."

That's bullshit," I said. "Only an idiot would service all the cooling pumps at the same time. And if they're being serviced, why aren't they locked into the off position and tagged?"

"Sergeant, tell Dr. Pearson we understand, thank him, and hang up," Lt. Clark said coolly.

"What?!" I gasped. I couldn't believe this guy was just going to let the reactor meltdown.

"This is a military operation, Rachael," Clark said, then nodded at Holmes. "Sergeant."

The Sergeant did as he was ordered and hung up.

"Now," Clark said. "My understanding is that situations in a nuclear power plant take hours or days to develop. Rachael, how long do you estimate until the situation becomes critical?"

"Give me a few minutes to check the readings," I said swiveling the camera on another circuit of the control room. "Well, I'm no expert, but based on the amount of water left in the core, the decay heat, and how much the temperature has climbed since the alarm went off, I'd say four hours before the core is exposed."

"Good. We don't know what Dr. Pearson is up to yet, and we need that time to figure it out."

The alarm klaxons were still going off outside our little room. The sound was starting to worm into my brain. I could see the bright white emergency strobes flashing through the crack below the door. Minutes went by. Finally, Dr. Pearson silenced the alarm.

We waited.

About fifteen minutes later, the alarms started going off again. I swiveled my camera around until I found a new set of flashing lights. "Feedwater pumps to the spent fuel pool are shut down," I said.

"How urgent is that?" Lt. Clark asked.

"Well, not very, yet."

"Time frame?"

"Could be days. The spent fuel is cooler than the fuel in the core, and there are thirty feet of water on top of..." I zoomed in on the water gauge for the spent fuel pool. It was dropping. "Um, the water in the spent fuel pool is going down."

"What does that mean?" Lt. Clark asked.

"Without knowing how or why the water is draining, or the flow rate, I couldn't tell you," I said. "It doesn't make sense to me. Those spent fuel pools aren't meant to be drained. It has to be sabotage."

"Leave the why to me, Rachael, you just keep telling us what's going on."

"What's going on," I said, "is that we're looking at a nuclear disaster that's going to make Chernobyl look like a gender reveal party, and we're just sitting here watching it happen."

Entry 32

"That is a radiation Klaxon," Lt. Clark said into his radio. "Strike teams to the emergency bulkheads."

I sat in the little dark security office staring at the screens in disbelief. The water level in the reactor continued to drop. The water level in the spent fuel pool was still dropping too. And the temperature in the reactor was rising and no one was doing anything about it.

Cassie was there with me. She'd been looking over my shoulder but hadn't said a word.

Sergeant Holmes pursed his lips. His brows drew together creasing to form an 11 in wrinkles above his nose.

The LT. running things, was cool...too cool. He just stood there. The place was on its way to becoming a nuclear hell and he acted like he was standing in line to order a sandwich.

After a few minutes, Dr. Pearson shut off the new set of alarms as well. We were getting closer to meltdown in the reactor, and the water in the spent fuel pool was still going down. Why wasn't anyone doing anything about this stuff? It made no sense.

"I need to use the ladies room," I said standing up.

"Now?" the Lt. asked.

"Yes, now." I crossed my legs.

I looked at the door.

"What?" he said.

"I don't feel safe," I said in as scared a voice as I could muster.

"Young lady, I have two strike teams on sight. You are as safe as you'd be in your mama's arms."

"This is an inside job. Anyone could be out in the hall waiting to take me out." I did my best to look innocent and doubtful at the same time. I think I deserve an Oscar.

"Oh Jesus Christ, Private, take Rachael to the ladies room."

"Yes, Sir," Cassie said standing up.

We walked down the hall and into the bathroom.

"This isn't right, Cassie," I said as soon as the door was closed.

She held a finger to her lips and checked the stalls. "No shit. Fucking place is going to hell."

"No, I mean Lt. Clark. I think he's in on it. He's dirty."

"How do you know?"

"Well, he's not asking the right questions. He just wants to know how long until shit really goes down. He's not asking how we fix anything. He's not taking the control room with the strike teams."

"Well, he could have a plan he's not sharing. The Army's like that, you know, Rach. But your right, he's not asking the right questions."

"What do we do?" I asked. I rolled my ankle a little to feel that reassuring weight of the Beretta strapped to it.

"We go along for now."

"We can't go much longer without getting water to the core and spent fuel pools. Do you trust that Sergeant?"

"Yeah, I trust him. Holmes is a good man." Her eyes gleamed bright and sure, drawing me in.

"What?" Cassie asked, her voice soft and familiar, as if she already knew what.

I wanted to tell her how I felt. How my stomach got all queasy when she looked at me. But this wasn't the time. Part of me wondered if there ever would be the right time for me to tell her. I switched my mind back to the business at hand. "Any way for you to let Holmes know that Lt. Clark is in on whatever is going on?"

"Holmes is probably way ahead of us on this, but I'll try to have a word with him if I can. We'd better get back."

When we got back to the security office, I sat back down and looked over the control room on the monitors. I could see Lt. Clark's reflection in the darkened monitor that usually showed the parking lot. He kept checking his watch.

"Looks like the water level in the spent fuel pool has stabilized," I zoomed in the camera on the gage in the control room.

"Good," Clark snapped.

"There's a vehicle on the access road," Cassie pointed to a truck coming down the road on the screen.

"Why is that monitor black and white?" I asked.

"It's dark out," Sergeant Dreamy said, "the camera switched to infrared."

The truck that passed the camera was a flatbed with two casks for spent fuel storage, and a dozen men on it.

"Son-of-a-bitch!" the Sergeant said, "I know what they're doing!"

"Huh?" I didn't get how he figured it out from that.

"Start a nuclear accident so that the strike teams are in their emergency shelters. Then steal all the spent fuel you want and then blow up the plant so that no one knows anything was taken. It just looks like a nuclear accident."

"Then what are the empty casks on the truck for?" I asked. "They've already got two ready to load here in the plant."

"They'll need to find pieces of cask when they investigate, or they'll know casks are missing."

"Sergeant, that is one amazing deductive leap. I'd like to put you in for a medal when this is over," the Lt. said, "but I'm afraid it will have to be awarded posthumously."

Lieutenant Clark drew his pistol and shot Sergeant Holmes in the head.

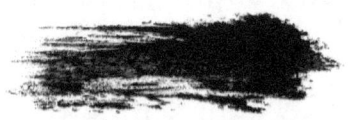

Entry 33

The gunshot thundered through the tiny security room.

I clasped my hands to my ears. "What the fuck!"

The Sergeant's body crumpled to the floor, blood oozing from the bullet hole in his forehead.

"Nice and easy now, ladies." The Lieutenant pointed his gun at Cassie and me.

Cassie stared at the Lieutenant through narrowed eyes.

"Private, slowly remove your sidearm and set it on the floor." The Lieutenant waved his gun at her hip.

Cassie did as she was told, never taking her eyes off of the Lieutenant.

"Now slide it over here with your foot."

She did.

He held his gun in one hand and pulled some plastic cuffs from his pocket with the other. He tossed the cuffs on the floor in front of us. "Put them on each other. Keep your hands in front of you where I can see them."

I reached down, my hand straying to the pant leg that hid my little Beretta. Cassie shook her head slightly, so I picked up the cuffs instead.

Once we were cuffed, the Lt. fiddled with his radio then keyed his mic. "This is Lima Charlie. Righteous. I say again: Righteous." His radio crackled with several responses: "Charlie Tango copies." "Sierra Charlie copies," that was Dr. Pearson's voice. "Sierra Foxtrot copies," that was Ron's voice. There were two more "copies," but I didn't recognize the voices.

I tried to hide my tears with my hands. I felt sick. I turned in my chair so that I didn't have to look at the Sergeant's body, face up on the floor with a hole in his smooth black forehead. His boots were still in view no matter how I turned in that small room. I half wondered why the Lieutenant hadn't shot Cassie and me, but I was afraid of the answer.

As if he'd been reading my mind, the Lieutenant reached out and wiped a tear from my cheek, then licked his finger. "Rachael, your innocent tears are delicious."

I bent down to get the Beretta from under my pant leg.

Cassie kicked me. When I looked up at her she mouthed: "Wait for your moment."

That did me good. The urge to cry evaporated. My stomach settled, and my fear vanished. My only thoughts were centered on how and when I was going to kill this son of a bitch.

We watched on the monitors as the empty casks were brought into the spent fuel area. Ron was oblivious. He stood on the control bridge over the pool working the controls of the crane, lifting the fuel rod assemblies into the submerged storage cask. The process was slow and boring to watch, like golf on TV. The robot crane worked precisely, lifting each spent fuel assembly out of its holder and into a receiver inside the giant yellow cask.

The radio spat out chatter as the troops not involved in the heist grew restless in their emergency bulkheads. The Lt. assured them that the levels of radiation inside the plant were too high to permit them to exit.

It took Ron hours to get the spent fuel casks loaded. Finally, the crane picked up the thick steel lids for the casks and lowered them into the water.

"Lima Charlie, this is Sierra Foxtrot Papa, ready to start the clock." It was Ron's voice.

"This is Lima Charlie. You are go to start the clock." the Lt. said into his radio. He reached down to his watch but stopped mid-motion staring at the monitors.

I turned back to the screens to see what he was looking at. Someone was slinking across the bridge behind Ron. As the Lt. reached for his radio again, the person ran up behind Ron and hit him on the head with a pipe. Ron crumpled onto the handrail. The man grabbed him and shoved him over the rail into the spent fuel pool. The person turned and flipped off the security camera. It was Phil.

"No, no, no, God damn it. Fuck!" the Lt. screamed. He keyed his radio and started barking instructions.

I pumped my cuffed fists over my head. "Yeah!"

On a different screen, another figure, I was pretty sure was Sylvie, hurried down the corridor, punched in the code, and entered the power plant control room.

"Pearson, look out!" the Lt. shouted into his radio.

The warning came just in time for Dr. Pearson. He whipped around with a pistol in his hand. Sylvie had a pistol of her own. The two stared down each other's gun barrels.

"Shoot her!" the Lt. screamed into his radio.

No one moved on the screen.

I felt a tug on my ankle. My pant leg lifted.

The Lt. stared at the screen and shouted into his radio.

The weight of the little pistol lifted from my ankle. Cassie came up holding the gun with her cuffed hands at the same time the Lieutenant reached for his gun.

Entry 34

No one ever thinks to pat down a 'help-less' young person. Especially a nerd like me. I'd worn the little Beretta on my ankle every day since Cassie gave it to me. It sucks too, because I have to wear army pants from Ft. Walters and not the jeans that Cassie bought me at the PX.

While the Lieutenant watched Ron get nu-clear waste swimming lessons from the guy on the bridge over the spent fuel pool, Cassie grabbed my gun. By the time the Lieutenant got his gun out of the holster, Cassie was already pulling the trigger.

She shot him right in the chest.

"No!" he wheezed.

He fired, but his shot went wide.

Cassie shot him again, in the throat. His blood spattered on the screens showing the security camera feeds, then ran down in slow syrupy drips backlit by liquid crystal.

The Lieutenant's gun went off again. The bullet whizzed by my ear close enough for me to feel the wind it made. The Lieutenant crumpled to the floor scrabbling at his throat.

Blood spread on the tile in a wide circle around him, then he lay still.

"Rachael, we have to go," Cassie said as she cut her plastic cuffs with the Lieutenant's pocket knife.

I stared dumbly at the bodies, then turned away to look at the bloody screens. The door to the spent fuel pool area opened and the truck rolled the empty fuel casks into the room. There were soldiers on the truck too; they pointed their guns at the man on the bridge over the pool.

On the screen showing the control room, Dr. Pearson and Sylvie both fired their pistols, and both went down.

"Rachael, come on!" Cassie cut the cuffs from my wrists and grabbed my arm.

"Sylvie," I sobbed as Cassie tugged me into the hall. I followed her down the corridor in a daze, the Lieutenant's blood spattered on the screens over and over in my mind. I saw flashes of the gunfire in the control room, saw Sylvie fall. My feet fell on the tiles numbly, one after the other. "Where are we going?" I asked.

Cassie wasn't listening. She was trying desperately to get the soldiers from her unit to answer the radio.

They weren't.

"Cassie, where are we going?" I gasped as we ran.

"We've got to get my teams out of the radiation bulkheads so we can save this plant. The radio must not be penetrating all the shielding between us."

That didn't seem right to me. Lieutenant Dickhead was able to talk to them okay. I didn't have time to argue about it though. "I have to get to the control room and get some water going into the core and the fuel pool."

"The hell you are," she grabbed my arm. "You're coming with me."

"Cassie, if we don't get that water flowing soon we're in real trouble."

"Real trouble?" her stride faltered for a second, "so, up till now, it's been just what? Alternative trouble? Besides, we need help. Come on!" She yanked me forward again.

We wound our way out of the power plant's control block and into the maze of controls, electrical panels, and stairs that made up the auxiliary building.

Cassie slowed to a stop and peered around a tall metal cylinder to see the door of the safety bulkhead. "Oh no! No, no, no!"

I moved to where I could see what she was looking at. The heavy metal door of the bulkhead stood open, scorched black.

"Wait here," she said. She made a crouched run, holding her pistol in front of her. She stopped with her back to the concrete just outside the door. She peered in quickly, then pulled her head back, once, twice, and went in.

A few seconds later she ran back across to me, her face drawn tight, eyes narrowed. She held a machine gun.

"Cassie, what—"

She held up a finger, bit her lip, and handed me back the Beretta. "They're dead. Let's get you to the control room."

We started working our way back to the control block. Cassie ran from one bit of cover to another, checking, then motioning me forward. The auxiliary building was quiet. Our footfalls rang out on the concrete sending echoes chasing each other through the tangle of pipes and machines.

My heart raced. And even the gun's cold metal handle couldn't steady my shaking hands. Occasionally I heard a faint shuffle or clink of metal hitting metal. Could have been anything, but my mind made it a bad guy just out of sight. I swung my gun wildly at each sound.

The door to the control room block lay just ahead. Cassie ran ahead to check it out. When she entered the code on the keypad, I felt something hard pressed against my back.

"Don't move. Don't speak," Dr. Pearson whispered. "I will kill you, Rachael, but I'd rather not."

"The way you killed Sylvie?" I hissed.

"I said don't speak," the gun, I assumed it was a gun, pushed into my back a little harder. "Hold up the gun, finger off the trigger."

Fuck it, I thought, at least I can save Cassie. "Cassie, look out!" I shouted. Then my world went black.

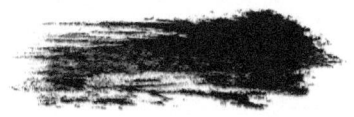

Entry 35

Pain screamed in my head. My temple throbbed in agony. The world heaved up and down. When I opened my eyes, I realized the world really was heaving up and down-upside-down. I was over someone's shoulder. I tried to look up to see who, but it made my head swim and ache. My stomach heaved.

My carrier grunted with effort. It sounded like Cassie, but I wasn't sure. Whoever it was wasn't tall, judging by how close my fingertips were to the ground. I decided the best thing to do was to play dead, which wasn't far from the truth anyway.

My hair felt wet.

Drops of blood trailed away on the cement floor behind us. My blood.

"Too many MRE desserts," Cassie grunted, then shifted her shoulder painfully into my belly.

"Shut up," Dr. Pearson barked.

There was the sound of a door opening in front of us. I recognized it as we passed through. We were in the spent fuel pool area. I felt the humidity from the warm water on my skin.

"Take the girl. Bind them both, hands and feet. Be careful though; I don't want them damaged any more than they already are." Dr. Pearson ordered.

Someone lifted me from Cassie's shoulder, cuffed my hands behind my back, and bound my feet.

They did the same to Cassie and sat her beside me, leaning against the wall. On the other side of me, Phil slumped hands behind his back, blood on his shirt. I wasn't sure he was still alive.

I turned my head back to Cassie. The room swam around me. Warm wetness ran down my face. "I'm sorry, Cassie," I said.

"No, I'm sorry. I tried to keep you safe. You should have gotten on the chopper."

A soldier with a machine gun kicked Cassie's feet. "Shut up!"

I looked out over the spent fuel pool. Dr. Pearson stood on the control bridge. One arm hung limp at his side. A soldier next to him helped him operate the crane. I could see a bit of Ron's leg floating on the surface of the pool. I wondered how radioactive he was now. The water prevented radiation from entering the atmosphere, but the water level was low, and he was much closer to the tops of the fuel assemblies than he'd be if there were thirty feet of water on top of the highly radioactive spent fuel.

"Phil," I whispered, "are you still with us?"

He grunted. That was good, but he didn't say anything.

"Phil," I kept at it, "Phil?"

The soldier that kicked Cassie came by and kicked me. "Shut up. I won't say it again. I'll just bash in the other side of your head."

I turned away from Phil to watch what was happening in the rest of the room. A spent fuel storage cask broke the surface of the water on the end of the crane. Men in radiation suits began hosing it down as it moved slowly toward the waiting trailer. Closer to us on our side of the pool other men were loading sacks of ammonium nitrate into an empty spent fuel storage cask. The crane set the dripping cask of spent fuel onto the trailer, and the men secured it. Then the crane lifted the heavy steel lid onto the cask of ammonium nitrate. Wires trailed out between the lid and the cask, and I wondered how they were kept from being crushed by the lid, which must weigh a few tons.

"Make sure the shims are fitted to those wires exactly, and the lid isn't too tight," Dr. Pearson called from the bridge.

There was my answer.

The crane picked up the cask with the ammonium nitrate and the wires coming out—now a giant bomb, and lowered it into the pool in place of the cask that just went on the trailer. Men on the side fed out more wire as the heavy yellow box disappeared under the water.

They repeated the process; a second cask landed on the trailer and a second bomb went into the pool. A big army truck came in, hooked up to the trailer, and pulled it out of the building.

I sat wondering if they were going to leave us there to die in the explosion, or if there was an even more nasty fate in store. My answer came a few minutes later when soldiers carried us into a vehicle that looked like a tank, but without a big gun. Once we were in the tank thing, the door closed and we started moving. Dr. Pearson lay on the floor, and a medic cut away his shirt.

"Corporal West," Pearson called over the din of the engine and clanking of the tracks, "how much time is left on the clock?"

"Three hours, twelve minutes," came the reply from up front somewhere.

"We've got to haul ass, Corporal; melting fuel rods are not like melting ice cream cones."

"Yes, sir."

A French-accented voice came through the radio over our heads: "Mayday, mayday, mayday. I don't know if that is ze right thing to say. Emergency! This is the Sea Ridge Nuclear Power Station. We have an emergency!"

Entry 36

"**S**ylvie!" I cheered.

"Ow," Dr. Pearson tried to get up, but the medic pinned him to the rattling floor of the Armored Personnel Carrier.

"It's through and through. Seems like the bullet didn't hit anything major, now hold still while I patch you up."

Sylvie was still on the radio talking about the status of the plant.

"I shot that bitch," Dr. Pearson sneered, "what's she doing on the radio?"

"Guess neither of you finished the job," I said.

"Do you want to be gagged, Rachael? Shut up. Corporal, can we jam her?"

"Jam her? In this heap? We're lucky we can hear her. These old M113's don't have much of an electronics suite, not like the Strykers," the Corporal called back.

"Damn it. Get on the radio and talk over her then!" Pearson shouted.

I looked at Cassie.

She looked at the floor.

They'd cuffed us with our hands behind our backs this time, and my shoulders hurt. Each time the tank thing hit a bump, my shoulders screamed in pain. It was nowhere near as bad as the pain in my head from where I'd been knocked out.

When the medic finished Dr. Pearson got up and sat across from us; his arm in a sling. "See what you can do for him," he pointed at Phil with his good arm. "He might still be useful." Pearson looked at me and smiled. "You haven't asked why you're still alive. You and your friend," he pointed at Cassie.

I said nothing. I figured it was best. I didn't want a gag, and I didn't want to play whatever game this was.

His grin broadened. "It's because you're delicious." He licked his lips.

My stomach did a somersault. Somehow I knew... but I didn't allow myself to even think it.

Cassie didn't look up.

I looked Pearson right in the eye, unblinking.

"You can wipe that self-righteous look off your face, Rachael. You think I'm some kind of monster, but you don't even know who you're working for. Do you know who is running Fort Walters? Or the Southern Survivor Colonies?"

I didn't, and it must have shown on my face.

"No, you just took what you could get. The first help, the first meal. Ate without question. They are not the legitimate government of the United States. I serve at the pleasure of the President. The PRESIDENT, Rachael. The people who run your precious Ft. Walters and the survivor colonies to the South are led by Franklin Walsh, the Secretary of Agriculture and a few dissenting generals." He swept his hand across the inside of the armored personnel carrier, "we are patriots, trying to restore the rightfully elected government of the United States."

It sounded like bullshit to me. First, the president had the flu. I heard at Ft. Walters that they found a treatment after just about everyone was dead. I also heard that people who got the treatment 'weren't right' afterwards. They had to be in separate colonies because of emotional problems. I thought the president was an asshole before the flu. If rumors were true, I hated to think what he might be like now. Still, I wasn't immune, if you'll pardon the term, from Pearson's argument. I really had no idea who was running things, only that they were good to me, and so far as I knew, weren't blowing up power plants on purpose.

That got me thinking about Sea Ridge reactor 1. No one ever really explained how it blew up. I'd just assumed that in the chaos of the pandemic there was no one there to take care of things; not until the Keeper Corps got there.

To my left, the medic was working on Phil. Phil's face looked gray in the light of the medic's headlamp, and the medic's face was grim. "What's our ETA?" he called up front.

"Twenty-fifteen hours," came the reply.

"I'm not sure he's going to make it," the medic said to Dr. Pearson. "I can't stop the bleeding." To Phil, he said: "I'll give you a little morphine. Make it a little easier."

"Don't make it easier for him!" Pearson shouted, his face an ugly purple under the blue lights. "He's a traitor, and he fucked everything up."

"We've got company," the driver's voice called from the front.

"Already?" Pearson asked. He looked at Phil, Cassie, and me. "This is your fault."

"That should be a little better," the medic said to Phil as he packed things away into his medical kit.

"We'd be free and clear if it weren't for you three and that French bitch," Pearson jabbed a finger at us.

"You'd have gotten away with it too, if it weren't for us meddling kids," Phil mumbled through a morphine haze.

Pearson picked up the radio mic. "You are harassing a United States Government convoy, this is the President's Science Advisor Dr. Randal A. Pearson speaking. Cease and desist immediately."

"I don't care if you're King Henry the fifth. You have sabotaged a United States nuclear facility and stolen nuclear materials. That is an act of terrorism. Stop at once," the radio crackled back.

"I have wired Sea Ridge Nuclear Power Plant to explode, the aftermath of which will make Chernobyl look like a glass of spilled milk. I say again, cease and desist." Pearson released the talk button on the radio mic and smiled.

Entry 37

"Corporal," Pearson called to the driver, "what do you mean 'we've got company?'"

"Two Blackhawk helicopters and two Apaches. If they wanted, they could blow us to hell right now."

Pearson grabbed the radio mic again. "Pull those choppers back or I'll blow Sea Ridge Nuclear Power Station right now."

"Dr. Pearson," the radio replied, "this is General Pike, Commander United States Forces South. You are ordered to stop immediately, surrender, and turn over the stolen nuclear materials or we will open fire."

"Are you willing to risk Sea Ridge blowing up, General?"

"Dr. Pearson, Sea Ridge is the only thing keeping you alive right now, blow it and we'll open fire immediately."

"General, I'm not stupid. I didn't set one bomb at Sea Ridge, I set three. You are in a position to determine how much of the Eastern Seaboard is destroyed. I'd suggest none."

No one spoke inside the armored personnel carrier for a time. The only sounds were the rattle of the engine and the clank of the tank tracks. We winced with every bump, Cassie and I because our wrists and arms were cuffed behind our backs and Pearson from the gunshot wound in his shoulder. Only Phil seemed immune to the jostling. His head lolled on his shoulder.

"The helicopters are breaking off," the driver reported.

Dr. Pearson sagged in his seat. He looked at Cassie and me. "It didn't have to be this way you know. I had the explosions calculated exactly. Minimal fallout, minimal contamination beyond the powerplant. All we were going to do was disguise the fact that spent fuel was missing. You and your friends fucked everything up."

"Bullshit," I said, "You were going to restart the plant. I saw you looking at the procedures for reactor restart. I saw you!"

"Do you still believe that, Rachael? After all this?" Pearson chuckled. "Do you know how long I had to sit at that computer staring at those startup procedures? Waiting for you to walk by? God, it was so boring. I had to do it over and over to make sure you saw me. All you people had to do was get on that damn chopper and go home. After the minimal explosions, you'd say I was trying to restart the plant and it must have exploded. I'd be presumed dead, and it would be one hundred years before it was safe to go into that plant and have a look. I'd have my spent fuel, and we'd all live happily ever after."

"Until you set off the dirty bombs you're making with the stolen spent fuel," Cassie spat. She'd been quiet since we were captured. I was beginning to wonder if she was okay. "If you have the President and the armed forces except for a few renegade generals as you say, why do this? If you are on the side of the rightful government, you have all the resources you need. What do you want with spent fuel if you have all the resources of the military at your disposal?"

"I'm not going to discuss that with a prisoner being held for treason." Dr. Pearson moved to cross his arms but realized that his arm was in a sling.

I had a hard time holding in a laugh. "Corporal?"

"Yes, sir?"

"Have the team on the flatbed check the external temperature of the casks."

"Copy."

We traveled in silence. I was anxious to know the temperature of the casks too. I wasn't sure what the temp was supposed to be, but my guess was not much more than 100°F. I wished I'd studied more about dry spent fuel storage systems, but since dry storage wasn't in the plan for Sea Ridge, it was deemed a waste of time. All I knew for sure was that metal containers were inches thick and could survive prolonged fire and planes crashing into them like 9/11.

"They say one fiver zero degrees," the Corporal called back.

"Time to destination?" Pearson asked.

"Two hours forty-five minutes."

"That's too long Corporal. We need the contingency cooling stop."

"Copy contingency stop," the Corporal replied.

I knew Dr. Pearson stole hot spent fuel, maybe even OCP 1, the hottest and most radioactive. Hot spent fuel needed water pumped through it constantly to keep it cool, like a car engine, otherwise it would melt and start outgassing hydrogen. Mix hydrogen with fuel rods melting at, uh...I forget, over a thousand degrees, I think. Anyway, it's bad. If the outside of the casks were one hundred and fifty degrees and the cask walls were a few inches of steel, the inside must be very hot. Add that to the fact that we were almost three hours from our destination, what you get is either a stop to cool the nuclear fuel or a very big explosion that would kill everything for miles around, especially us.

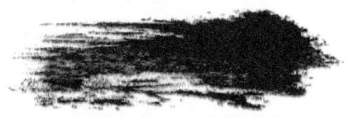

Entry 38

I'd lost all feeling in my hands from the cuffs. My shoulders screamed in agony from having my arms pinned behind me for so long. Every bump of the armored personnel carrier sent a fresh wave of pain through my limbs.

Cassie wiggled beside me. I figured she was trying to get circulation going again in her hands. On the other side of me, Phil was slumped back against the side of the APC. His chest rose and fell. His eyes were closed. His mouth hung open. I was scared he'd die and slump over on me; then I'd have to ride with a corpse resting on my shoulder.

Funny how after all the death I'd seen since the pandemic started, the prospect still upset me. I figured at a certain point I'd just be numb. Sometimes at night I still see all the faces of the dead flashing behind my eyelids.

We stopped. My ears rang in the silence. It's odd how you don't realize how loud and annoying something is until it stops. In this case, it was the squealing and clanking of the APC's tracks and the roar of its engine.

The medic came over and started checking Phil. He shook his head and mumbled to himself as he went about his work.

I wiggled a little in my seat trying to get the blood flowing back in my hands below the plastic cuffs.

Dr. Pearson stopped at the door. "Corporal, check their bonds." He pointed at Cassie and me. "we don't want our prime breeding stock getting loose."

I wanted to kick him! Breeding stock! He was talking about us like we were cows! It must have shown on my face because Pearson laughed.

"You didn't think we were keeping you around for your nuclear expertise, did you?" He opened the rear door of the APC and went out into the night.

I never wanted to kick someone's ass so badly in my life. I vowed to myself that I was going to get that son of a bitch if I ever got loose.

The Corporal came over, reached behind Cassie first, then me, and tugged on our handcuffs. Then, he too, stepped out of the APC.

"How is he?" I asked the medic working on Phil.

"He isn't getting any better. I don't know if he'll hang on long enough to get where we're going." He strode out the door without a look back, leaving Cassie, Phil and I alone in the APC.

"You okay Rach?" Cassie asked.

"Yeah, my hands are all pins and needles, and my head is killing me from where Pearson thumped me, but I'm okay I guess."

"We've got to stop these guys, Rach."

"We've got to get loose first. Maybe ask to use the bathroom?"

"I doubt that'd work. If I were them, I'd tell you to just piss your pants. If they do let us pee, they won't undo the cuffs, they'll just undo your pants. If you're lucky that's all they'll do, but I wouldn't count on it."

"Gross." I shivered.

"Exactly. Anyway, there's a bolt behind me. I've started rubbing the plastic on it. It's going to take a while, but I think I can break the cuffs before we get where we're going. What we have to figure out is: once I'm free, how we stop them and then escape. That's where I'll need your help. I don't know anything about all this nuclear stuff.

"I barely know anything about it," I said, "I've only been studying for a month, and I didn't study spent fuel dry storage."

"Well," Cassie grunted as she moved her wrists back and forth behind her, "you know more than me."

"Yeah." I had no idea how to stop them. I leaned forward trying to see what was going on outside. It looked like a hotel parking lot. I could see trucks parked all around what I guessed was a swimming pool. There were deck chairs piled up in the corner. One of the trucks, a tanker, had hoses going into the pool. Steam rose from around the hoses. I couldn't understand why they were using something hot. Then I realized that the steam wasn't from something hot, it was from something very cold.

As I watched, a crane lowered the casks of spent fuel into the water. Billowing clouds of steam rose as they went in. Big waves of water the casks displaced rolled over everything. "This is going to take some time, I think. The water won't be deep enough to shield everyone from a massive dose of radiation. That means they won't be able to open the casks to cool them. Even if that water is ice cold, it will probably take hours for the cold to get through the thick steel walls of the casks."

"No one is watching us," Cassie grunted, working her arms faster, trying to break the plastic handcuffs. "We might be able to make our move here."

"Okay," I said. I was thinking about something else though. Something Phil said about the thick steel pipes at the power plant. If you heat them too fast, they crack. I wondered if that worked for cooling them too. If you cooled the hot steel casks too fast, would they crack?

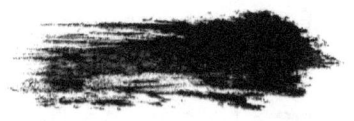

Entry 39

As I sat in the armored personnel carrier, I squeezed my hands together to get the blood flowing below the plastic cuffs. Cassie's arm movements set me jiggling as she tried to saw through her cuffs with a bolt behind her. It made my vision double occasionally as I watched steam rise from the hotel pool where the casks of spent nuclear fuel were cooling.

Hoses ran from a tanker truck into the pool, and the clouds of gaseous water rose from where they entered the water. I thought of my inspection tours with Phil at the nuclear power plant, and his voice echoed in my head: You can't heat them too quickly. If it's cold on the outside, and hot on the inside, the metal won't have time to expand. It will crack.

I thought about how cold they were making the outside of the casks, and how hot the casks must be on the inside. "I think they're playing a dangerous game," I said. I had to shut up quick because I heard something outside the open door of the APC. I kicked Cassie, and she stopped wiggling her hands.

The driver poked his head in. "You okay in here? You want a glass of wine? Pedicure maybe?"

"Fuck you," Cassie spat.

The Corporal laughed and disappeared again.

Cassie returned to cutting her plastic cuffs on the bolt. I returned to thinking about how to stop these assholes from getting their spent nuclear fuel.

"You were saying something about a dangerous game?" Cassie's voice vibrated in time with her wiggling arms.

"Yes, I think they're cooling the outside of the casks too much too fast." I told her what Phil said about the pipes cracking.

I looked over at Phil. His eyes were closed. His chest rose and fell slowly. "Phil, PHIL! Come on, wake up! We need you!"

He didn't move.

"It's not fucking working. The bolt just isn't sharp enough to cut these cuffs," Cassie grunted.

"We've got to get out of this. We've got to stop them!"

"No shit Rach, just how do you propose we do that?"

The sound outside changed. Above the sounds of the men talking, and machinery humming, I heard the sound of distant helicopters. "You hear that?"

"They're coming," Cassie said gravely.

"They're coming for us!"

"No, Rach, they don't know we're alive. They're coming to wipe these guys out."

"Well, that's pretty good right?"

"Not for us, Rach. This APC will be one of their first targets. We have to go now."

"Not like this!" I wiggled the hands cuffed behind me, but Cassie was already pushing herself to her feet.

"Shut up and follow me."

I had a hard time getting to my feet with my hands zip-tied behind my back, but I managed. Cassie was already at the door when Dr. Pearson appeared.

"What the F—" he grunted and toppled over from the savage kick Cassie delivered to his balls.

The radio in the APC started going crazy with chatter that I didn't understand. Gunshots peppered the night. They grew more intense until it sounded like popcorn.

"Come on Rach," Cassie yelled.

I felt the wind from a bullet whiz by my head. "They're shooting at us!"

"No shit. Go!" Cassie dashed out into the night.

I kicked Pearson in the head as hard as I could, feeling his soft melon give, then I followed Cassie as best I could. I didn't have any time to take in my surroundings. All I could do was follow her into the battle. We ran awkwardly, arms behind our backs along the sidewalk in front of the hotel. Bullets hissed past me. Something exploded behind me, but I didn't dare turn around.

We made it to a spot behind some abandoned cars in the parking lot of the restaurant next door. I risked a look back. There was a smoking hole next to the pool where the casks were cooling. "Holy shit! They're aiming at the casks!" I panted.

"Let's go!" Cassie sprinted for the restaurant.

I sprinted after her. We squatted down behind a bush in front of a little brick alcove.

"Maybe we can find a knife inside."

"No time. We're too close," she said, then she broke cover and ran again.

The fight seemed to be mostly behind us. I couldn't hear bullets in my ears anymore. As we ran behind the gas station next to the restaurant, something bit into me. I fell.

Entry 40

I sprawled on the pavement behind the gas station. My arm screamed in agony. Something wet and sticky running down my sleeve. Cassie sprinted away, unaware I wasn't behind her. Swearing, I tried to get up, but my arms were still cuffed behind my back. I rolled over on my good shoulder and tried to get my feet under me.

Coppery blood filled my mouth, dripping from my face. I realized that the pain in my arm was masking the pain in my face from where I'd fallen on it.

"Rachael!" Cassie called from the next building over.

"I'm here," I yelled as I got to my feet.

"Come on!"

"I think I'm shot," I called as I ran toward the sound of her voice.

"Run!"

I got to her just as a helicopter passed overhead.

"We got lucky," she panted.

"You call this lucky?" I moved my shoulder toward her. My shirt was black with blood in the darkness.

Cassie squinted at it. "Looks like just a graze. Hard to tell. We've got to move."

"We've got to get out of these cuffs," I said. It wasn't clear in the darkness what kind of building we were hiding behind. What was clear was that it was the last building before the highway interchange. I could see the ground sloping down to the road below. The dark silhouettes of abandoned cars stood out against the night.

"No cover for one hundred yards," Cassie said, catching her breath. "You any good at the hundred-yard dash in school?"

"Downhill with my arms cuffed behind my back?" I pictured myself pinwheeling down the slope.

"No choice," she said.

"They haven't hit the casks with the spent nuclear fuel yet." I looked up the slight rise to where the firefight raged near the hotel pool.

"And they haven't hit us yet—" Cassie began.

"Speak for yourself," I said, thrusting my bloody shoulder at her.

"These guys hit what they aim at. In their scopes, we'll look like enemy combatants hiding out. We have to go. Come on!" With that Cassie got up and started running.

I followed. Just as I reached the grassy slope down to the highway, the ground shook. A concussion wave from a big explosion knocked me off my feet. I fell on my wounded arm, screaming in pain. Hot pieces of something fell from the sky. Whatever it was burned holes in my clothes, my hair, everything. I rolled onto my side and looked back. The hotel pool was a smoking ruin. They'd hit the casks.

I struggled to my feet; a tough and painful job with the cuffs on. It hurt everywhere. In the back of my mind, I knew if I'd been peppered with exploded, highly radioactive pieces of nuclear fuel I was already dead. In the front of my mind, there was only one thought: RUN!

The grass on the slope was slippery with dew. I fell and rolled down the hill. When I got to the bottom, Cassie's voice came out of the darkness.

"Over here," she called from the underpass. She was climbing up the cement slope under the bridge.

I scrambled after her. At the top, Cassie hunched in the shadows, her hands still cuffed behind her. She was looking up into the beams.

"No way to climb up there like this," she said. "Why are you way over there?"

"Cassie, I have a problem."

"Rach, what is it?"

"You need to stay away from me."

"Are you hit? Again, I mean?"

"No, Cassie, they hit the casks. Debris landed all over me." I could barely talk I was crying so hard. "I'm dead!"

Entry 41

C assie took a step toward me. "Rachael, you're not dead. You don't know what kind of debris fell on you. All kinds of debris come from an explosion."

"Maybe." My tears fell onto my shirt. I couldn't wipe them. "It was probably radioactive. I have to get out of these clothes, I have to scrub."

"Okay." Cassie looked down at the abandoned cars on the road below. Light from the distant battle flickered on the dusty windows. The sound of gunfire and helicopters sent thundering echoes under the bridge.

"Stay here." Cassie made her way down the cement slope of the underpass and nosed around the cars tucked into the deep shadows. She found an old car, turned around, and pumped her arms obscenely up and down. After a minute or two she raised her arms in triumph. She rooted around in the car for a minute, then ran up the slope toward me.

"Turn around." She cut the plastic cuffs.

Fresh pain erupted in my wrists and shoulders. I stretched and worked the blood back into them. I began to cry again, half from the pain, half from the fear of being radioactive. I started tearing my clothes off and throwing them as far away as I could.

"Rachael, you can't just be naked out here." Cassie looked shocked.

"Those clothes are poison!" I shouted. "Every second I'm in them I'm getting more radiation!"

"You don't know that."

"Yes, I do!" I stood naked and shivering under the underpass. "I need to wash," I sobbed. I bit my lip. I had to get myself under control. I had to get tough.

"I don't know how to help you with that right now."

I stood on the slanted cement, naked except for my shoes. The pain of the burns on my head, back, and the backs of my legs cut through my fear. The bullet wound on my arm throbbed. Blood trickled from it and dripped black on the cement in the darkness.

The sounds of battle died down, then stopped altogether. Helicopters flew away into the night, then it was quiet.

"We should go," Cassie said.

"Is it safe?"

"Is it safe to stay?"

"No," I said, "I think we need to be further from the radiation."

"I'm worried about you running around out here naked," Cassie said.

"I'm shot, burned, radioactive, bleeding, and you're worried that I'm naked?"

"Yeah, okay, Rach lets go."

"Which way?"

Cassie didn't answer; she just hurried down to the road, turned left and started jogging. I ran after her, holding my braless chest in place.

The highway exit we'd come from was apparently the last bastion of civilization heading in that direction because there was no sign, literal or figurative, for anything else. I was scared, cold, and in pain. All I could do was concentrate on my feet. Step, step, step, step.

Diamond-shaped orange signs appeared on the other side of the highway, followed by lines of orange cones. The cones guarded some kind of construction site. Bulky shapes in the gloom resolved themselves into all kinds of construction vehicles.

"Over here," Cassie called as she crossed the median.

I followed her up to a truck with a tank on the back. "Gasoline?"

"Water," she said, "for keeping the dust down. Let's hope it still has some in it."

"We need something to scrub with, a brush or something," I said, looking around.

"You want me to scrub your burns with a brush?" Cassie was incredulous.

"No!" I was doing a great job of holding back my tears. "But it has to be done."

"Okay, wait here." She ran off into the dark.

"Where would I go?" I muttered.

She came back a minute later holding a bunch of stuff. "Jackpot."

The only thing I could make out in the dark was a broom. "You're going to scrub me with a construction site broom?"

"Yeah well, these guys don't keep loofas in their trucks, and you said it has to be done. I'll wash it first. Best we can do. I also got a tarp for you to lie on and some coveralls for you to wear after."

"You could fit two of me in those."

"Okay, stay naked then," she spat.

"Sorry. I'm scared, naked, and I hurt so frigging bad."

"I know," she said as she spread the tarp on the ground.

The truck had water in it. Once Cassie washed the broom, I lay on my belly under the spigot. I yelled when the icy water cascaded over my body. The broom hit my back. Pain stabbed its claws into my spine as Cassie started scrubbing. I cursed her. I told her I hated her. I screamed. The pain was worse than anything I'd ever felt. I passed out.

Entry 42

Pain. I became aware first of the pain in my back, then my arm, then the pain in my legs. I opened my eyes to a view of pale dawn casting its light over a yellow truck. My view was partially obscured by hair tickling my face, hair that wasn't my own. I was draped over Cassie's lap like a child, chest to chest, my head resting on her shoulder. Sick as I was, I couldn't help thinking that this was what I'd wanted for so long—to feel Cassie close to me—but not like this.

My stomach churned; bile rose in my throat. I moaned into Cassie's shoulder.

"You back with me?" Cassie whispered.

"Uh-huh."

"How you feelin'?"

"Awful."

"Yeah, you had a rough night."

"I need to puke," I mumbled, trying to untangle myself from the foil blanket wrapped around us while holding the meager contents of my stomach down.

"Go easy," she said.

The world spun as I lifted my head from her shoulder. I leaned over and threw up all over

the controls of the machine we were in. "Sorry," I whispered, then spat bile from my mouth.
"It's okay, but let's get out of here. The smell is making me want to puke too."

The cab of the machine was tiny and cold. There was barely room for me to climb off her. She helped me figure out how to open the door. I tried to make my body turn and climb down the ladder to the ground, but my limbs didn't seem to work right, and I tumbled out of the backhoe into the cold dirt.

As I started to pick myself up, I felt the stiffness of tape and bandages on my wounds. "Bandages?" I croaked.

"Yeah," Cassie said climbing out of the backhoe. "You passed out when I was cleaning you up. I found a first aid kit in one of the construction trucks. I did a hurried patch job, but I was worried about the cold. We should take another look at you in the light, but first, we've got to get some water into you."

My tongue lay thick in my mouth. I tasted vomit.

Cassie put her arm around me and helped me stumble to the tailgate of a nearby pickup truck. I sat on the edge so that the wounds from burning shrapnel weren't taking my weight. Cassie poured some water from an orange cooler into a white cone-shaped cup and handed it to me.

"Why a backhoe?" I asked when I'd finished my water. "Why not lie down in the cab of this truck?"

"The backhoe had a smaller cab. Better chance of holding our body heat. I needed to hold you for us both to stay warm.

"Thank you." I tried to smile.

"Shut up and drink more water," she said, taking my cup and refilling it.

"I'm cold," I said, taking the cup from her.

"As soon as you're hydrated, we're going to work on that."

"Why bother. Fatigue, vomiting; I've got acute radiation sickness. I'm a dead woman."

She stood in front of me, arms folded, eyes narrowed. "Don't ever fucking say that again. Those are also symptoms soldiers experience after action, and you've seen a lot of action. No more negative talk. No giving up. We're survivors. We survived the virus. We survived the battle. We survived the explosion, and we're going to survive this. We go down the list of priorities in order: Water, shelter, food, communications, transport. Now drink up."

I sipped the water from the cone cup. It was cold. I was cold. I didn't really want it.

Cassie got the foil blanket from the backhoe, washed the puke off it at the water truck, shook it out, then wrapped it around me. My stomach wobbled around in my guts. My head ached, and the burns on my back throbbed.

I tossed the water cup into the bed of the pickup and looked down at the greasy blue coveralls I wore. "How did you get me dressed and into the backhoe?"

Cassie smiled. "It wasn't easy. Let's just say there was nothing dignified about it. How are you feeling now?"

"Cold, sick, I've got a splitting headache, and everything hurts. I feel like I'm getting the flu."

"Wouldn't surprise me," Cassie said, "running naked in the night then scrubbed with cold water, maybe dehydrated too. Drink one more cup of water for me, then lie down in the cab of the truck. I'm going to see if I can get one of these vehicles going, or get a radio working so I can call Ft. Walters for Evac."

I did what she said even though I didn't want the water. The truck smelled like grease and stale cigarette smoke. I wrapped myself in the blanket. The sunlight through the windshield felt good on my face.

I woke up sometime later to the sound of the truck's door opening.

"How you doing, Rach?"

"I...I don't know." I sat up, fighting my way out of the sleep-fog. "A little better, I guess."

"Think you can walk for a while? I couldn't get any magic happening here. Looks like we're on foot until we can find something."

"I'll try." The foil blanket made me sound like a bag of potato chips trying to climb out of the truck. We walked through the loose brown soil of the construction site and out onto the highway again.

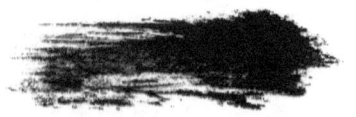

Entry 43

The October sun warmed our faces as we walked south on the highway. My feet dragged with fatigue on the unforgiving pavement. The burns on my back and the backs of my legs throbbed under the bandages. The cuts on my face itched in the sunlight.

We stopped at every stalled car on the highway, corpses or not, to see if they would start. None did, so we searched them. We found some bottled water in an old Plymouth minivan and granola in a Subaru. My stomach heaved with every step, but I knew Cassie would force me to eat if I refused the food. I pretended to eat and stuffed the granola bar in the pocket of my greasy coveralls. I wasn't in my right mind. I knew that much. The world swam around me. My thoughts jumbled in my head. All I could do was pick up my feet and put them down again. It felt like I was dying. I wanted to say so. I wanted to tell Cassie to just let me go, let me lie down on the grassy median and become one with the sky, but I knew she'd just yell at me.

I sat down in the road while Cassie checked out some old orange Toyota shit box we'd never get running.

"Jackpot," Cassie said. "Any chance you can drive a stick shift?"

"I once backed up a dump truck in a hurricane," I said.

"So, not really." She looked into the car, then at me. "It'll be okay. I'll talk you through this. Come sit in the car."

I did.

"Okay. Left pedal is the clutch; you push it in and I push the car. When I yell, you let it out fast. The car will start to buck. Give it gas. That's the pedal on the right."

"I know," I said. I didn't like her talking down to me. My head was pounding. I just wanted to lie down.

"Good. Once the car starts, push the clutch in again and hold it, then hit the brakes.

I tried to focus, tried to remember the order of things. It seemed simple, but I felt terrible. "I'll try," I said.

"No sweat." She put on a forced smile and closed the door. From the back of the car she yelled, "clutch in, foot off the brake." Then she started pushing the car. It rolled very slowly at first, then faster, and faster still.

"NOW!" she yelled.

I couldn't remember what I was supposed to do for a second, then I took my foot off the pedal. The car lurched and sputtered.

"GAS!" Cassie yelled.

I hit the gas. The engine seemed to catch for a second. The car jerked to a stop.

"Okay," she huffed alongside the driver's window. "I think..." She gasped. "...this will work if we give it one more try. I just need a second," —gasp— "to catch my breath."

She caught her breath, and we did it again. This time the engine caught.

"Clutch in!" she called.

I put the clutch in. The engine kept running. The car kept going.

"Brakes!" she yelled. "Keep the clutch in!"

I did what she said. The car kept running.

She opened the passenger door and jiggled the shifter, then pulled the hand brake. "Thank God. You can relax."

Cassie drove. I lay in the reclined passenger seat. The day wasn't particularly hot. It was October after all, but I was hot. I lay sweating on the cracked vinyl. The world wavered in and out.

"Hey, Rach, how you feeling?" Cassie's voice floated to me from far away. She was like an angel. The sun setting behind her bathed her in a golden halo.

"I've felt better," I said. Everything hurt.

She put a hand on my forehead. "Jesus, you're burning up."

The world receded. When I floated back, she looked down at me.

"Don't worry, Rach, I have a plan. Just hang on a little longer."

The world receded again.

Her voice penetrated the nothingness.

"Rach..."

I opened my eyes.

"We're at a truck stop. I need to go inside. Whatever you do, don't shut the car off. Understand?"

I doubted that I was even strong enough to sit up and turn the key. "Uh, yeah."

A sound woke me. Cassie was back. The driver's door was open. She popped the hood. "Almost home, Rach," she said, then she was gone again. Well, not gone. I could see her fiddling around under the hood for a while. She closed it, but not all the way. She ran some wires and laid them on the hood. She set a box there and began to unpack it. It was a CB radio like truckers use. She fiddled with it for a minute, then grabbed the mic and said, "Fort Walters, this is Kilo Charlie One Two, do you copy?"

Entry 44

The radio crackled static back at Cassie. She knelt on the pavement of the truck stop parking lot, adjusted the dials of the CB radio and tried again. "Fort Walters, Fort Walters, this is Kilo Charlie One Two, do you copy over?" Again, there was a burst of static. "I thought we'd be in range." She dumped the radio in my lap and jumped in the driver's seat. "Keep trying. Don't give our exact location until I talk to them."

"That won't be hard," I whispered. "I don't know where we are." My head and hands felt heavy, stuffed with cotton.

"Yes, say that stuff. We are Kilo Charlie One Two. Got it?"

"Yeah."

"Good. I'm going back in to get a few things."

I kept trying on the radio, doing my best to remember all the words, but all we got was static.

Cassie came back with a basket full of stuff: sports drinks, all kinds of granola and protein bars, and a map.

Even though I couldn't remember the last time I'd eaten, I just wasn't hungry. I looked at the protein bar Cassie forced on me, but I couldn't bring myself to eat it.

"You have to eat," she said.

"I'll throw up."

"Just take a little nibble for me, okay?"

I did. It was gross. I drank a whole bottle of orange sports drink, then tried the radio again.

Still nothing.

Cassie traced her finger over the map. "The radio isn't powerful enough to reach Fort Walters, but it might reach one of the listening posts we have set up along the I-95 corridor. I got stuck on that boring ass assignment a couple of weeks ago while you were at the power plant. We should be in range in just a few more miles.

I felt like I was going to throw up again and my burns were screaming agony. "Cassie, I really don't feel good."

"I know, Rach, I know. We'll get you to the hospital soon." She put the car in gear and headed toward the highway.

I was in and out of the brain fog for a while. Sometimes when I opened my eyes Cassie had the microphone, calling out as she drove. Sometimes she was squeezing my hand. Once I saw her looking at me crying.

"Lima Papa Three Baker, this is Kilo Charlie One Two, do you copy?" The frantic tone of her voice snapped me back to reality.

The radio crackled: ...ma...pa three...b...er, go ah..."

"Come on, come on..." Cassie muttered through clenched teeth. She tried again. The response was still garbled but clearer. Cassie responded with our code name, then said: "We are four miles northwest of your position on the Niner-five, request emergency medical evac..." She gave a description of the area, the car, and my initials. She finished with "acute radiation poisoning, over."

"It's just the flu," I croaked.

"Ssshh, Rach."

"Kilo...arlie one...oo, we copy...and by."

"What's all that mean?" I asked. I didn't get the jargon at all.

"They said they got it, and to hang on."

I slumped back in my seat. They heard us. Then a thought struck me: "How come we didn't just go to the listening post?"

"Well, one, the location is a secret, and two, it's a three-mile hike up the side of a mountain."

"I thought we weren't supposed to tell our location on the radio, you know, in case the bad guys are listening?"

"I only gave our location in relation to the listening post, which is secret. The bad guys will have to search miles of highway for an orange shitbox, and the choppers will be here by then. You rest now, we're almost home."

The radio crackled back that the choppers would be there in twenty minutes.

Cassie copied them, then held my hand and stroked my hair. "It's gonna be all right now, Rach."

"I know," I said. "It's just the flu."

"Yeah," she sobbed, "sure." She stopped stroking my head. I opened my eyes. She held her hand up in front of her. It was covered with my hair.

Entry 45

The chop of an approaching helicopter brought me back to reality. It roared into the twilight, thundering in my ears. The wind the chopper kicked up as it landed on the empty freeway blew dust and trash in through the open door as soldiers carried me away from the car.

As soon as we were on the chopper, they started sticking needles in me. Cassie told them about the burns on my back and legs. They turned me over. I'd been in kind of a stupor until they ripped the bandages off.

I screamed.

"We're going to give you something for the pain now," a voice said.

There was a needle jab, then the lights went out.

I woke up in a fogbank. Whites and greens and fuzziness. I felt pain far away. It was quiet. We were not on the chopper anymore. I felt someone squeezing my hand.

I opened my eyes.

Cassie sat next to me in a hospital gown.

"Hey, Rach," she said softly. "Welcome back."

"Hey," I whispered, groggy and weak. My throat was a desert. I tried to push myself up, but my arms were like overcooked noodles. I managed to roll onto my side to look at Cassie.

"Watch the plumbing," she said, indicating the tubes and wires coming out of my arm and going to a bunch of bags and machines next to the bed.

Cassie's eyes were red and puffy. She sniffed, wiped her nose on the side of her finger, and smiled at me. "How ya feelin'?"

Good question. I didn't know. I felt the pull of taped on bandages on my back and legs. I still felt weak, tired, and foggy. "Thirsty."

"Here," Cassie handed me a cup with a straw.

I drank it dry.

"You've been crying," I said.

"It's nothing; just overtired." She wiped her eyes and put on what she thought must be a reassuring smile.

"Where are we?"

"New Hope Hospital."

New Hope was the name of the survivor's colony right outside of Fort Walters. The base had a clinic, the one I went to when I got to Fort Walters, but there weren't enough doctors to go around, so the tough cases went to New Hope.

"You're a patient too?" I asked looking at her scrubs.

"Yeah, just a little radiation. I'll be fine."

"That's good." The word radiation brought everything home; the station, the fuel rods, everything. "How's the power plant? Did the bombs go off?"

This time Cassie's smile was genuine. "No, Sylvie saved it."

That made no sense to me. "How? Dr. Pearson shot her in the control room. I saw it on the monitor."

"Don't you remember the distress call we heard in the APC? Remember how pissed off Pearson was?"

"Ah, it takes more zan a little bullet to stop me." Sylvie's French-accented voice came from behind me.

"Sylvie!" I tried to turn over to see.

"Watch the plumbing!" Cassie grabbed my arm and fixed the tubes so I didn't rip them out.

"You made it!" I smiled at her. "And you saved the plant! It's so good to see you, Sylvie. How'd you do it?"

"After that bastard, Pearson shot me, I was how you American's call playing possum. When I 'eard Dr. Pearson leave, I call for 'elp and started the water flowing to ze core again. Helicopters came, disarmed the bombs, and brought me here. Now I have ze sexy scar on my shoulder."

"That's amazing," I said. "I can't believe they disarmed the bombs in time."

"Well," Sylvie smiled. "I suppose they wanted plenty of time to get clear of the radiation zone, so they set a long delay on ze bombs. With no one alive in the plant, it would have worked."

"Except for you," Cassie said, her voice choked with emotion. "You saved the day."

"No, we saved ze day. You and Rachael, and ze soldiers." Her voice broke. "And Phil." She looked away.

Phil. I'd forgotten about Phil, and I felt terrible about it. Phil stopped Ron from loading the spent fuel into the casks. Even though Dr. Pearson finished the job, Phil slowed them down, gave us time to try to stop it. "So he..."

"Rachael, he was in the APC when the casks blew. Even if he could have survived the gunshot..." Cassie's voice trailed off.

The room was silent for a long time. I tried to lie on my back, but my burns were just too painful, so I rolled onto my stomach facing Cassie and fell asleep.

I woke to whispers sometime later:

"There must be something else we can do," Cassie whispered. "She didn't even ask about herself. She asked about everyone else, even that fucking power plant. She doesn't deserve this."

"Private," a man's voice, clinical sounding, said, "It's not unusual for someone at this stage of radiation poisoning to appear to recover and then..."

"And then?" Cassie whispered angrily.

"And then relapse," the man whispered. "We are doing everything we can for her at this time. It's touch and go, but she's young, and before this, healthy. We just have to wait and see."

"How long till you're sure?"

"A few days, but I warn you, even if she recovers, her chances of getting cancer within a few years—"

"No!" Cassie whispered. "I cleaned her up as soon as I could, scrubbed her down—"

"You performed admirably under extreme circumstances, but the damage was done long before you scrubbed her down. Anyway, we'll know in a couple of days."

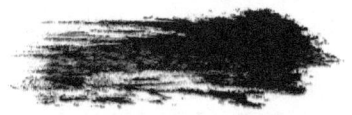

Entry 46

I had no concept of the passage of time in that hospital. It was like swimming underwater. Sometimes I'd come up for a breath of air and Cassie would be sitting in the chair next to my bed. Once in a while, she'd be gone. Sometimes I drank from a straw she held for me. Sometimes we'd talk a little, but most of the time she just squeezed my hand. Once I woke to her crying. I pretended to be still asleep until I really was.

The next time I woke, the mind-fog was gone. The burns on my back and legs were only irritating instead of painful. I was *hungry*. Not like normal hungry where you buy too much at the grocery store; I was 'gnaw on a dead gutter pigeon' hungry.

Cassie slept in the chair next to me, her head tipped back against the wall, mouth open, snoring. I held in a chuckle. I didn't want to wake her. Making sure not to 'rip out the plumbing,' as Cassie would say, I grabbed the tubes and wires coming out of my arm and quietly maneuvered myself into a sitting position. It was hard. I was weak, but I knew...I was back. I was going to be okay.

I was super thirsty too. There was a half-finished coke next to Cassie; I drank it. It was flat and warm, but it tasted oh so good anyway. A nurse walking by saw me sitting up and started to say something. I held a finger to my lips and pointed at Cassie. The nurse smiled and nodded. I made eating motions with my hands. The nurse held up a finger and hurried away.

It took a while, but the nurse came back with a tray of chicken, green beans, potatoes, and Jell-O. Even after the apocalypse, hospitals have plenty of Jell-O. I gobbled it all down like I'd never eaten anything before in my life.

I wanted to let Cassie sleep, but I got bored. No TV because, you know, the apocalypse. No books around my bed either. Just as I opened my mouth to wake Cassie, a doctor came in.

"Well, Rachael," he said, "how are you feeling?"

"Good," I said, "hungry."

Cassie grumbled and opened her eyes.

"Appetite is a good sign."

"Rach!" Cassie leaned over and gave me a squeeze. "Yay!"

"Watch the plumbing," I chided playfully. "So, when can I get out of here, Doc?"

"Slow down, Rachael. We'll do some more tests, and if everything looks good, maybe the day after tomorrow."

"What?" I felt fine. I was ready to go. I wanted Cassie's couch and lousy cooking, and DVDs! Then I thought of the conversation I heard about radiation patients relapsing. "Are you afraid I'll relapse?"

Both the doctor and Cassie looked surprised, but the guy was cool. "It's a remote possibility, but I think you're past that stage. Your appetite is a good indicator. No, I want to keep you to make sure your infections are totally gone. The burns on your back became quite septic."

"What's my prognosis long-term?" I asked, remembering hearing something about cancer.
"You are at a significantly increased risk of cancer. You'll need frequent checkups. You may yet lose some fingernails."
"What?" I didn't like that. It sounded gross and painful.
"It won't be as unpleasant as it sounds, and they'll most likely grow back—"
"Most likely!" I interrupted.
The doctor kept going, "—as will your hair."
"My hair!" I touched the top of my head: skin. "This sucks!"
"You're lucky to be alive," the doctor said. "Lucky to have a friend as resourceful and caring as Cassie. She saved your life."
"She's not my friend," I said.
Cassie looked shocked and hurt.
I grinned. "She's my family."
Cassie punched me in the arm, then hugged me.
"Careful," the doctor said, "she'll bruise easily for a while."
"Great."
"I knew you'd pull through," Cassie said, releasing me. "You're a tough bitch. Now I can tell the Colonel that you can see him. He's been up my ass about you for a week."
"A week? How long have I been here?"
"Almost two weeks."

Entry 47

The doctors say that I can't work at the power plant anymore. I can't risk accidental radiation exposure. I have to limit things like dental x-rays. I have to cover up completely when I go out in the sun. This sucks. I'm bummed because I felt like I was starting to understand things at the power plant. I liked working out the math of things and imagining the way the neutrons moved inside the reactor. I have no idea what they're going to ask me to do now. I know they're going to ask me to do something though. I signed up for a five-year hitch in the Keeper Corps. It's hard to believe that I've only been with the corps for a few months. In that time, I've learned about nuclear power, spent nuclear fuel, and power plant operations. I've been a part of stopping the theft of several tons of spent nuclear fuel. I've been shot, blown up, irradiated, and scrubbed naked with a construction site broom. My hair has fallen out, and now so have my fingernails. My fucking fingernails! If I ever get to the survivor colony it's going to be hard to get a date. When the doctor said my hair would most likely grow back fine, I wanted to punch him. MOST LIKELY!

The worst thing is that so far no one will tell me about who Dr. Pearson was working with. He claimed he worked with the legitimate government of the United States. He claimed that the President was in charge. It makes no sense. If that is the legitimate government, why were they trying to steal spent nuclear fuel? The real US government should be up to its ears in all the nuclear materials it could ever use. I mean, don't we have enough nuclear bombs and missiles to destroy the world several times over? What do they want with spent nuclear fuel?

There is something else that's bothering me. All this time I've never been to the survivor colony. No one on base ever talked about it. Even here in the hospital, no one talks about it, and we're right on the edge of it.

I have heard about the treatment for the flu. The people here call it the smiling flu because of the way people get punchy and happy before they go into the coma, and because of the way you smile when you're in the flu coma. I never really saw it myself. My brother locked himself in his bedroom when he got really sick. Sometimes if I've had a bad day, I see his grinning corpse peeking from under the sheet I wrapped him in when I dragged him from the apartment. I see all the rotting faces looking at me from the stalled cars along the road.

I feel like there's something else about all this they're not telling me. It seems like there is some big piece of the puzzle that they're holding over my head and I don't understand why.

I'll tell you this: before I accept another assignment, before I lift another finger to save this sorry world, I'm going to get some answers. After all, I've been through, I think someone owes me at least that.

They are supposed to release me from the hospital tomorrow. I guess I'll stay with Cassie in her apartment on base until I get a new assignment from the Keeper Corps. Cassie went back to her duty assignment yesterday. They've given her stuff to do around the base until I'm well, so that's pretty cool.

I'm getting stronger and doing just about everything for myself. The Band-Aids on my fingers that cover my missing nails are super annoying. They make it hard to button my jeans. Yeah, I got most of my stuff back from the power plant. There was no radiation in the control block, thanks to Sylvie. She got released yesterday. She's in charge of the Sea Ridge Nuclear Power Plant now; so good for her, I guess.

Anyway, they said my sneakers were radioactive. I don't know why, but I find that funny; radioactive sneakers. Sounds like a band name. And now, ladies and gentlemen, the Radio Active Sneakers doing their latest hit: Scrubbed with a Broom. Cassie got me some combat boots for now, which I wear unlaced because they're hard to tie with these frigging Band-Aids on my fingers.

Tomorrow, before I'm released, I have a meeting with Major McShane. Remember, he's the one that gave me the assignment at the power plant? I guess he has some questions for me.

I'm not telling him shit until he tells me about the government and what's so secret about the survivor's colony.

Entry 48

I went to the second-floor conference room in the personnel building of Fort Walters at ten o'clock in the morning. My unlaced combat boots shuffled on the dull green floors. I was pretty nervous because I knew they were going to ask a lot of questions, but I was determined not to tell them anything until I got some answers about what the hell is really going on around here.

The bandage from my middle finger that covered my missing fingernail caught on the handle to the door and started to unravel. As I wrapped it back up, I saw Major McShane sitting at the conference table talking to my doctor, Dr. Chu. They were looking at some papers in a blue folder when I walked in.

"Rachael," McShane said, extending a freckled hand, "good to see you up and around." He smiled. "Coffee?"

"Oh god yes," I said as I shook his hand. I was a little surprised. I expected him to act mean and start grilling me right away.

The Major poured me some coffee from the carafe on the table behind him while I said hello to Dr. Chu and shook his hand. McShane handed me a Styrofoam cup and sat back down. "First," he said, rubbing the red hair that ringed his bald head, "I want to thank you personally for your service to this country. You acted bravely and honorably. We're still working out medals and honors for the Keeper Corps, but you are first in line to receive one once we have it squared away."

"Thank you," I said. "The real question is: what country are you referring to? Dr. Pearson claimed to be working for the real US Government. He said he was working for the president and the Chairman of the Joint Chiefs of Staff. If that's true, who are you working for? What government is this?"

"It's complicated," McShane sighed, "there are a lot of factors involved here. We are the good guys and that's all you need to know for now. I want to talk to you about—"

"I'm not telling you shit," I cut him off. "Until you tell me who I'm working for."

"Settle down Rachael. I'll explain, but it's complicated."

"I've got plenty of time." I tried to sip my coffee casually, but my hand was shaking a little and I burned my lip. "Ow, fuck."

"Okay." McShane suppressed a smile, "I'll humor you. You've been through a lot. Dr. Pearson wasn't lying about working for the President and the Joint Chiefs, but he was lying about them being the legitimate government of the United States."

"Huh?"

"The President had the Smiling Flu," Dr. Chu said. "As did the Chairman of the Joint Chiefs. And almost everyone in the bunker. When the treatment was developed, they were among the first to receive it." Chu looked uncomfortably at McShane, who nodded for him to continue. "There is a problem with the smiling flu.

You see, the flu virus is coated with proteins that help it infect the host. This flu has an extra protein. The extra protein affects the brain's pleasure center, overloading and overwhelming it. In a way, the effect is very similar to heroin. That's why flu victims go into a coma. In so doing, burned out the brain's pleasure center. People who recover from the flu and the coma... they are different afterward."

"What? Like zombies or something?" I asked. This was getting weird. I pictured the survival colony full of zombies from books and TV.

"No." Chu smiled. "Nothing like that. They can no longer feel pleasure, joy, reward, or anything like it."

"So you see," McShane cut in, "the President, whose judgment was questionable before the flu, can't be trusted to make decisions without the capacity for pleasure or reward. He might just launch the nuclear missiles to end everyone's suffering. No person who has recovered from the Smiling Flu can or should be allowed to make decisions that affect the American people. The new government, the one that was operating while the President was in a coma, remains in control of most of our weapons of war, and the entire nuclear arsenal."

"Then who the fuck were all those soldiers with Dr. Pearson?" I asked.

"In any situation like this, there will be factions that don't go along. They call our government the product of a coup d'état. They follow the President and the Chairman of the Joint Chiefs blindly. Fortunately, most of the surviving military are with us, but it's going to take some time to bring these rogue elements in line."

"Okay," I said. I trusted them. I had no choice, really. They'd been good to me and I had to trust my gut. "Now, what about the survivor colony? How come I've never been there? How come no one talks about it?"

"The survivor colony..." Major McShane sipped his coffee and cleared his throat. "The survivor's colony, New Hope, is right outside the hospital. There's nothing secret about it. You probably haven't heard much about it because most of the personnel on base don't go there. There's no reason to. At this point, everything from housing to shopping is better on base. The three thousand people that live in New Hope are still largely scavenging what they need to survive, and power isn't all that reliable yet. Life is simply better on base."

I leaned back and crossed my arms. "I'm not buying what you're selling. There are so few people left. Crappy or not, the soldiers I've met would go into town no matter how crappy it is."

McShane massaged his forehead for a moment. "The people who recovered from the smiling flu aren't just unhappy. They're different. Unpleasant. Hard to be around. Normal people don't want to go near them. And they prefer their own company. They say no one really recovers from the smiling flu. That's why its survivors call themselves... The Unrecovered..."

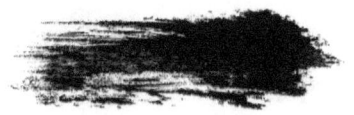

Also by

The Smiling Flu Series

Book 1 – *The Unrecovered*
Book 2 – *Rachael's Apocalypse Diary*
Book 3 – *Beneath the Dark Water (late 2025)*

Other Books by Len M. Ruth

The Pull
Tales of the Doomed

Stay Connected

Get the latest news, exclusive goodies, and free reads by signing up for Len's monthly newsletter:

About the author

L en M. Ruth writes unsettling fiction
about what haunts us—grief, memory,
and the fragile machinery of society. When
he's not working late in live show production,
he's crafting stories that blend quiet terror
with emotional depth. Len lives in Las Vegas
with his partner, Emory, and Cooper, the cock-
er-blocker spaniel. When not conjuring ghosts
and bad decisions, he's hiking desert trails or
plotting his next haunting. Find him at lenmru
th.com

www.ingramcontent.com/pod-product-compliance
Lightning Source LLC
Chambersburg PA
CBHW020121180626
46812CB00006B/2689